ALANA OAKLEY

mystery & mayhem

An imprint of Enslow Publishing

WEST 44 BOOKS™

Please visit our website, www.west44books.com.
For a free color catalog of all our high-quality books,
call toll free 1-800-542-2595 or fax 1-877-542-2596.

Cataloging-in-Publication Data
Names: Inkwell, Poppy.
Title: Mystery and mayhem / Poppy Inkwell.
Description: New York : West 44, 2020. | Series: Alana Oakley
Identifiers: ISBN 9781538384800 (pbk.) | ISBN 9781538384794 (library
bound) | ISBN 9781538384817 (ebook)
Subjects: LCSH: Detective and mystery stories. | Mothers and daughters--
Juvenile fiction. | School--Juvenile fiction.
Classification: LCC PZ7.I559 My 2020 | DDC [F]--dc23

Published in 2020 by
Enslow Publishing LLC
101 West 23rd Street, Suite #240
New York, NY 10011

Cover design and Illustrations: Dave Atze

Typesetting: Think Productions

Printed in the United States of America

CPSIA compliance information: Batch #CS19W44: For further information contact
Enslow Publishing LLC, New York, New York at 1-800-542-2595.

ALANA OAKLEY

Mystery & Mayhem

An imprint of Enslow Publishing

WEST 44 BOOKS™

by Poppy Inkwell

For Mum for teaching me how to read
my first word...

For Papa Bear for the words that made me
believe I could do anything...

And for Alex who embodies the most
important word of all...

ACKNOWLEDGMENTS

G is for the Girls who have felt **DIFFERENT**, weird or **alone** ... this book is for you.

R is for all the Random moments that make life *exhilarating*.

A is for the **Awesome** manuscript assessment service provided by Sean Doyle.

T is for the Terrific Team at **Big SKY Publishing**. Thanks for taking a punt on a square peg.

I is for the artists, designers, writers and musicians who constantly INSPIRE me.

T is for **TALL** Tales and long noses ... infinitely more mesmerizing than the Truth ... or are they???

U is for my five, Unbelievably, Uber-cool children who are Unequaled in their Uniqueness. *Je t'adore!*

D is for my Dearest friends and family ... my creative **SOUL-MATES** ... the legwarmers of my h♥art.

E is for all the Exceptions to the rule. You **ROCK**!

Thanks . Gracias . Arigatô . Shukran .
Merci . Choukrane . Ďakujem . Danke .
Köszönöm . Terimakasih . Faleminderit .
Grazie . Xièxiè . благодаря . Nandri . Salamat .
Mahalo . 감사합니다 . Ngiyabonga . Ta . Diolch .
Շնորհակալություն . Obrigado . ευχαριστώ .
Dankie . Tänan . спасибо . Takk . Thankyouahh .

CONTENTS

PROLOGUE

1 September, Final Year of Primary School.

Alana Oakley dreaded her birthday. The *age* she was turning didn't bother her, but the trips to the hospital (or worse) did. Her birthdays, you see, always ended in catastrophe. She supposed it wasn't her mom's fault every celebration was ruined, but dancing llamas? Seriously? And the juggling fire-breather would have been more fun if Alana's hair hadn't caught fire. Maybe her mom *should* be held responsible – it was always her ideas plunging them into trouble in the first place – but you can't blame someone for Thinking Big and Having A Huge Heart. Or that's how Alana's dad explained it. Her dad ... Alana allowed herself a smile as she closed her eyes, just stopping short of wishing the obvious (one last kiss or hug from a father she missed so much sometimes she couldn't breathe), and blew out twelve candles ...

This time, I want my birthday to be different.

If she'd known how her wish was going to come true, she probably would have changed her mind ...

CHAPTER 1

Nail polish, handbags, and the ozone layer.

3 February, First Year of High School!

Alana Oakley took the stairs two at a time. She was ready extra early for school today, excited and nervous to begin high school. A tremendous thump accompanied her final jump onto the landing, prompting her mom, Emma, to look up from her computer.

Alana looked at her mother, who resembled her in so many ways. They shared almond-shaped eyes, although Alana's had flecks of hazel, whereas Emma's were a warm brown. Their flyaway hair stuck out at matching odd angles, and their skin was the same honeyed tinge. Alana loved the way her mom's skin smelled. It reminded her of sun-kissed peaches: sweet and fresh. It was the smell of home. The only thing Alana seemed to have inherited from her father were his dimples. They made her look like she was always up to something, even when she wasn't.

"You look nice, darling." Her mom took a second look, taking in the new uniform. "Oh no! It's not today, is it?"

"Yep. First day of high school, Mom. Remember?" But of course, Emma never did. Or if she did, she got the dates wrong. Important stuff, like when tax returns were due, or when school fees needed to be paid, seemed to fly right out of her head. Emma buried herself in her work like an archaeologist looking for treasure. Since the death of Alana's dad, Hugo, three years ago, things had become worse.

Emma's eyes rounded with shock as she clapped a hand to her mouth.

"I was sure it was next week. Have you got everything you need?"

Alana ran through the list of things she'd done: sat the entrance exam and achieved a scholarship for Gibson High. *Check.* Bought school supplies from the Orientation Day list. *Check.* Pumped bicycle tires. *Check.*

"Yep, all done, but I need to get going soon. I don't want to be late for school. I promised I'd meet Sofia and Madison, so we could go together."

Alana's circuitous route to meet her friends, Sofia and Madison, would take her from Marrickville to Redfern, then back to Newtown. It would take longer, but the three girls preferred to face the daunting task of Day-One-Year-Seven together than alone.

Sofia was the long-awaited daughter, after five sons. Alana had been friends with her since daycare. From potty training to trainer wheels, there wasn't a moment in Alana's memory when she *didn't* know Sofia. There'd been only one gap in their friendship: a year filled with youth hostels, backpacks, and living in a wildlife sanctuary deep in the jungles of Borneo. During that time, Emma's valuable research had forced people to stop logging, allowing corridors of forest for orangutans to live. Or that's how Emma described it. Alana had a very different memory of her mom chained to a tree and being groomed by enormous, ginger-haired primates as they exchanged bananas. Alana's grandmother went into a state of denial when concerned relatives called from the Philippines. "No, that's not Emmalina," she said. "It just looks like her." That was until Emma made the cover of *Timeless Magazine*. Gran had sung a different tune then. Emma's increased profile had certainly helped her get work, and she was usually swamped.

Alana met Maddie on the *Kidz2Air* program at the community radio station, three years ago, just after Alana's dad died. When the girls had met (Alana sad, bewildered, lost; Maddie confused, angry, frightened) there was an instant connection. Maddie shook off her fear to take Alana under her wing; she knew what it was like to lose a dad. Alana liked to believe both dads looked down at them from heaven, and met up sometimes to chat about *their girls*.

Alana couldn't wait to see her friends again. Summer had dragged its feet. Sofia had spent the holidays visiting two of her older brothers studying in Melbourne, while Maddie was at music camp.

"Thank goodness you're on top of it all. Hugo was always good at that kind of thing." Emma's eyes took on a wistful look.

A knock on the door interrupted them, followed by a loud, baritone honk. Alana rushed to the window. A tall figure with longish hair waited on the doorstep. In a Tolkein tale, he would have worn dark, leather riding gear, and wielded a sword. Instead, he carried a black, bulky bag which Alana knew would contain the latest DSLR camera equipment.

"Uncle James!" Alana yelled, as she flung the door wide. James was her mom's work partner. He took all the shots Emma needed for the articles she wrote. He often said they were like Bonnie and Clyde, to which Emma would retort they were more like Bert and Ernie. Emma was the best interviewer James had ever worked with. Her natural charm and vulnerability, was disarming and engaging. Even the most uptight of interviewees opened up like a flower, while with other journalists, they remained as silent as a clam. It was this talent he was counting on for their next interview, which promised to be HUGE.

Honk. Honk. "Heya, Pipsqueak. Ready for your big day?"

"Yes, of course. What's with the horn?"

"It was your mom's idea. She told me to get it for your first day of school. In case drivers give you grief on your bike."

"As if they'd dare!" Alana declared, hand on hip. "It's a nice idea, I guess … if I was five, or wanted to join the circus."

"She means well, Kiddo. Anyway, I thought you might feel that way, which is why I brought you this," he said, presenting Alana with a small box. "I believe it has GPS, some cool games, and it probably plays music. But no matter how smart these smartphones get, I still haven't found one that makes decent coffee."

Alana squealed with delight and hugged him while he pretended to gasp for breath. She rushed to show her mom. James trailed behind looking sheepish.

Emma pouted. "How come she gets all the cool toys?"

"Because I don't lose them like you do," Alana shot back.

James peered over Emma's shoulder at what she was working on.

"It was a freebie, Em. No big deal. You know I don't know how to use those things. Give me a normal phone any day. *Talking whale 'Nox' socks off in Australia*," he read. "What are you up to now?" He did a quick check of her internet surfing history while Emma tried to shoo him away. "You'd be a much better journalist if you didn't get so easily sidetracked."

Emma's response was to stick out her tongue.

"Very mature. I hope you haven't forgotten our meeting with Slam Guru today. I had to pull all sorts of favors to get an exclusive, and he *never* gives interviews."

Slam Guru was one of America's most successful rock stars. His debut single had shot to number one within days of its release. He was on tour, playing in London, Tokyo, and Prague, with performances scheduled in September for the Sydney Cricket Ground – a venue with a capacity of fifty thousand. The Sydney concerts sold out within hours. Unlike other artists who promoted their tours, Slam had one general press conference. He guarded his privacy fiercely. Bodyguards accompanied him everywhere and he never attended music awards. Slam Guru was a man surrounded by mystery. Emma's interview was nothing short of a scoop.

For the second time that morning, Emma clapped a hand over her mouth. "But I thought it was next month!" she wailed. "The girls are coming over to –"

But she didn't get to finish, because the very "girls" Emma was expecting arrived. Ling Ling Shu teetered in on bright, high-heeled, pink wedges. The baby-doll dress she wore was a perfect match for her cherry-colored hair. Her contact lenses magnified her pupils so much, Alana was reminded of an albino goldfish. Ling Ling, adorned head-to-toe in various shades of pink, looked out of place in the narrow, suburban hallway, as if she'd gotten lost on her way to a *K-Pop* performance. Blinking, Ling Ling's fake eyelashes became stuck. She tried to separate them, but her fake nails were too long. They sounded like crabs scrabbling in rock pools as they clicked together.

A second woman clunked through the door. Somebody had forgotten to tell her the Seventies were over. A neon orange tube top puckered limply around her flat chest above a pair of tightly-packed, flared trousers. Peacock-blue eye shadow made her already bulging eyes leap from her face like a pair of suicide skydivers. A long, thin nose cleaved her pale face into two, ending in a pair of pouting lips. The woman's figure was a classic pear-shape, blossoming like a gourd. But that wasn't how she saw herself. Every morning she squeezed herself into a size 12, her bottom always looking slightly breathless for doing so. At the sight of Alana, the woman's gaze narrowed. Katriona Karovsky was not the maternal type. She looked at children like they were bubblegum on the bottom of her shoe. They smelled funny, made too much noise, and were an awkward reminder of how old she was getting. To make matters worse, Alana was always annoyingly *sensible*.

"Been let out of your cage, then?" the woman drawled.

Alana rolled her eyes. Katriona Karovsky didn't scare her, and she wasn't afraid to show it. She pasted on a plastic smile.

"Oh hi, Auntie Katriona. Hi, Auntie Ling Ling. Sorry I can't chat about nail polish and hand bags, but I have to learn how to fix the ozone layer … especially since *your* generation has stuffed it up!"

At this, Katriona's pencil-drawn eyebrows disappeared into her hairline. She gasped like a fish out of water.

"*My* generation? I'm not that much older than you," she protested, but Alana was already out the door, farewell kisses flying to Emma and James.

Katriona had just finished composing herself when a loud *honk* made her stumble midstep. Alana's dimpled grin reappeared in the window.

"Thanks for the present, Mom. I can see it's going to come in real handy!"

Another loud *honk* had Katriona clutching her chest, before Alana pedaled off for Redfern.

CHAPTER 2

The definition of "hirsute" is not a pantsuit for women.

By the time Katriona and Alana finished exchanging insults, Ling Ling had managed to unstick her eyelashes. Now both were fixed to her upper eyelids like a pair of furry caterpillars. She blinked.

"What did I miss?" she said to no one in particular.

When nobody answered, Ling Ling peered through the thick fringe to see Katriona inspecting Emma's teeth with all the thoroughness of a vet with a horse. She checked under Emma's arms, glanced at her eyebrows, glared at her nails, tugged at her hair, and then took a vicious swipe at the hem of Emma's nightie. She crossed her arms with a look of disgust.

"Salon. Now." The tone in Katriona's voice brooked no argument.

Like many houses built during the 1930s, the semi-detached terrace which Emma and Alana called home was long, narrow, and dark. It was with great reluctance, therefore, that James stepped from the convenient shadows to protest.

"But she can't. We've got an interview with Slam Guru today."

In an instant, Katriona's demeanor changed. She raised one arm to clutch the doorframe, bent a knee, and thrust her hips forward. The other hand gripped her waist. Her silhouette resembled a rather large cello leaning against the door. James took a step back.

"James! Dah-ling!" she cooed, batting her eyes. "I didn't know you were here."

James gave a nervous smile as Katriona continued to use the doorway as a prop for her poses. She had a ton of them, and was eager to show the photographer every single one. She always hoped it would inspire him to take out his camera. So far he never had.

"Hang on," Katriona paused mid-pose, a Greek

statue giving directions. "THE Slam Guru? *Rock My World* Slam Guru? As in, *Lightning strike me down with your devil eyes.*" Katriona began singing Slam Guru's latest hit.

"Maybe a trip to the salon isn't such a bad idea." Emma shrugged, as James's eyes widened at Katriona's dancing. Her tube top shifted treacherously southward while her pants threatened to bust open with every shake. "Katriona *is* one of Slam Guru's biggest fans. She could bring me up to speed on his background while they fix me up."

Katriona's head bobbed as she bounced like a pogo stick. "Pleasepleasepleasepleasepleaseplease," Katriona begged with hands clasped together. She was almost hyperventilating in anticipation.

With a sigh, James gave in. "Two hours. Tops. But you *cannot* be late for this one."

Emma's promise was muffled by Katriona's triumphant screech of delight. She grabbed Emma's hands, jumping with childlike glee.

Ling Ling peered at Emma's hairy legs as the

skirt of her nightie flew up and down.

"Two hours is not enough," she said sorrowfully to James.

CHAPTER 3

Ready for anything... except snot.

Alana cut through the back streets of Marrickville to avoid as much traffic as possible. The morning rush hour was in full swing. The double-story Victorian semi's of Alana's neighborhood gave way to the terrace houses of Erskineville, and eventually the modern apartments characterizing the new look of Redfern, a suburb famous for its history of poverty and violence. During the day, shops displayed their wares, but dusk brought with it shutters and padlocks. As Alana passed the shopping district, the street was a patchwork of grey metal and black bars.

Alana's friend, Maddie, lived near an area known as The Block. She coasted down Eveleigh Street, carefully steering clear of stray dogs. Children playing in the street looked at her with curiosity. White girls on bikes didn't visit this part of town often, Eurasian ones even less so. It was known as a Tough Area, an area driven by a cycle of poverty that kept people down. When Maddie was born, and her mom held her, no more than a babe herself – she'd struggled for a name that would carry her daughter as far from The Block as possible. Far away from its sense of fear and hopelessness. There was power in names, power in words. Madison Square Gardens, New York, was what she came up with. The name "Madison" also meant "mighty warrior," according to an elderly German shopkeeper.

"Yep," Maddie's mom had warned the tiny bundle philosophically. "You got yourself a fight now, girl."

Alana braked in front of a Victorian house of dark red brick. It was one of a dozen identical buildings in various states of disrepair. Refurbishment hadn't reached this far yet. Some had broken windows. Others had no windows at all. Boards and bricks covered the gaps. Alana parked her bike before knocking. Slivers of peeling paint cascaded to the ground.

An Aboriginal woman in her late twenties opened the door. She was an older, plumper version of Maddie, with the same dark, curly hair, open smile, and eyes the color of shallow coral reef water. Alana was enveloped in a hug that she returned with equal warmth.

"Oooh, you got big," the woman said, looking Alana up and down.

"So did you," Alana replied with a cheeky grin. The woman laughed out loud and slapped Alana's back as she yelled over her shoulder.

"Ma-ddie! Alana's here!"

The announcement provoked a thunder of footsteps. Two children clustered by Alana's legs, clamoring for attention. Alana gave them both a cuddle.

"Green snot," said Cassy, who was two and a half, holding up a finger full of evidence.

"Is not. It's yellow," said her brother, Troy, a year older.

"Green."

"Yellow."

"Green."

The argument had Maddie's mom shouting about keeping snotty noses away from nice young girls, as she dragged the children away. No sooner had she got rid of one, however, than the other would return, and the process would start again. This prompted her to yell for Maddie in even greater earnest.

"I'm coming, I'm coming – " a girl's voice rang out.

Maddie bounced into the room and tackled Alana from behind in a wrestling move that had them both giggling.

"You ready, then?" Maddie asked her friend with a meaningful look. It was hard to say exactly what she was referring to. *Ready for what? School? New friends? Life?* In the mood Alana was in, she felt ready for anything … except maybe algebra.

"Bring it on!" Alana said with a serious look, sparking another fit of laughter from the pair.

"That's what I like to hear. Now you take off before these two notice," Maddie's mom said, jerking her head at the younger children eating breakfast. "And don't forget this," she said, passing her daughter a black violin case.

"Thanks, Mom. See you later."

"Yeah, see you later, Mrs. D."

The bang of the door alerted Maddie's younger brother and sister of their departure. Their scream of disappointment could be heard through the door.

CHAPTER 4

Sit. Roll over. Play dead.

Alana and Maddie made their way toward Redfern Railway Station on foot. Alana steered her bike with one hand. Maddie slung her bag on her shoulder and carried her violin on her back. The girls enjoyed a companionable silence. It was one of the things Alana liked about Maddie the most. Maddie didn't need to fill spaces with idle chatter. She understood that silence has its own special place.

The façade of Redfern Railway Station was the same dark red brick of Maddie's home. In the early morning sunlight, it revealed paler shades of apricot and orange under the billboard posters and graffiti tags that covered the surface.

A towering man stood outside the entrance. His shock of white hair showed up in sharp contrast to the earthy tones of the wall behind him. His wrinkled skin was the color of mahogany, eyes yellow with age. His hair was so bushy and wiry that it looked like a bird's nest. He leaned heavily on a crooked shopping trolley. It was as if all his worldly belongings were in that one metal cart. Flattened cardboard boxes were filed neatly on one side, to serve as bed and blanket in the evening. Maddie greeted him like an old friend.

"Hello, Uncle!"

Alana knew instinctively the man was not Maddie's real uncle. Just like James, Katriona and Ling Ling weren't her real relatives. Like her friend, Alana had been taught to address elders with respect. As a consequence, she had more "aunties" and "uncles" than was physically possible. The man responded with great animation, but made little sense.

"Thumbs and toes is all, I says. Seems plain to me, or any ordinary soldier."

"Too right, Uncle. Not too much to ask at all."

"Darned if I know what for," the man continued, and then shouted enough expletives to floor a truck driver. His shower of spittle darkened the sidewalk a slate grey. Several commuters gave him an even wider berth than his bulky form and belongings already commanded.

Maddie nodded in sympathy, then gave his arm a squeeze before turning to go. The man's eyes took on a sudden lucidity. He smiled, showing big gaps between his teeth.

"Bless you!" he said to Maddie, before launching a second tirade involving "prissy politicians" and "extra forks."

The girls made their way to the train on their platform. Sofia was already on, having come from Central Station. Her delicate hand waved them down to where they should get on. The carriage was already quite full. By the time Alana wheeled her bike in, there was little room left. Sofia moved her bag so Maddie and Alana could sit next to her.

Sofia was born with the kind of eyelashes Ling Ling would have killed for. Her dark eyes sparkled as she twisted strands of her waist-length hair, which was dyed varying shades of purple, around one long, slender finger. "Piano fingers," Sofia's father had predicted proudly, inspecting the long, spidery digits of his newborn daughter. "Drums?!" he'd cried, appalled, when Sofia chose her instrument years later. Because she was very superstitious, Sofia wore enough charms to knock out a vampire by sheer weight alone. Today an amulet of Ganesh – the Hindu god of happiness – as well as a Wu Lou pendant, for good health, hung around her neck. Her favorite charm was a Magic 8 Ball, which she consulted for even the simplest decision. The bright blue of her mood ring indicated she was feeling happy and sociable. It must be said, however, that Alana never saw it change color.

Even before the train lurched into its journey, the girls launched into an animated conversation, three multi-colored heads clumped together when the rattle and hum of the train got too loud. The seats were double-facing, bringing them face-to-face with a couple of hefty teens in Nike T-shirts and the latest high-top sneakers. The girls had a whole summer to catch up on, so it was easy to ignore the boys' stares and whispers, until one of them leaned forward. His pimply face inches from theirs.

"Betcha she stole it."

It was obvious the youth was talking about Maddie and her violin. The look on his face dared her to contradict him. Her response shot out like gunfire.

"What's that supposed to mean?"

He sat back, looking Maddie up and down, aware that the color had risen in Maddie's cheeks, and that her friends were bristling with anger.

"People like *you* don't normally own things like … *violins*, do they?" His friend snickered. They both thought the idea very funny.

If any adults noticed the exchange, they did not show it. People often ignore injustices for the sake of Not Getting Involved, too afraid of Making Matters Worse. Not realizing matters are made far worse because of it.

Before Maddie or her friends could respond, a

girl in the same school uniform as theirs pushed herself into view. She was a bit on the chubby side, and her black hair was woven neatly into a long, thick plait. A similar-looking case was slung over one shoulder, but hers had a *Muslims Rock!* sticker on it. With flashing eyes she pointed her own case at the boys, as if taking aim.

"Who said they were violins?"

For a brief moment, the boys exchanged that look of panic all bullies wear when someone calls their bluff. They watched movies – they had seen bad guys pull a machine gun out from where a guitar should have been. They could easily imagine a weapon lurking in the smaller cases – especially when the girl wielded hers as if armed. Maddie joined in the pretense, jerking the tip of her violin case upwards.

"*Bang!*" she mouthed.

To their credit, Alana and Sofia kept a straight face while the boys scrambled over each other to escape, not even bothering to retrieve a shoe when one fell off.

"See? Mine's a flute!" the fourth girl called out to the boys' fast-retreating backs.

It wasn't until the train was at Newtown Station that the four students could stop laughing long enough to introduce themselves.

"*Assalamualaikum.* I'm Alana. And these are my friends, Maddie and Sofia."

The girl looked taken aback as she shook Alana's hand.

"*Mualaikum salam,* Alana. I'm Khalilah. Nice to meet you Maddie, Sofia," but her curious gaze never left Alana for long, still surprised by the Muslim greeting of peace. Alana smiled and offered an explanation.

"I traveled around Malaysia for a year when I was little. I don't remember much. Just the food."

"Did you like the food?"

"Definitely!"

"Then you should come to my place one day. My dad cooks a mean *rendang* curry."

"*Fantastique!*" said Alana, who was learning a new French word every day, for when she visited

France to discover her "roots"… and other things related to her father.

There are some situations which bind people together forever. The death of a loved one. The birth of a child. A shared triumph. This was one of those times. The four girls smiled at each other, happy to have made friends even before they'd arrived at school.

CHAPTER 5

School loses its charm.

Gibson High lay nestled between Newtown's converted warehouses and the Police Boys' Club, a popular base for youth programs aimed at troubled teens. The school building itself used to be an old factory. Its design was made even more unusual by the inclusion of many original fixtures and features. The school's philosophy – that it should be a school *for* the community, *by* the community – began with the first brick that was laid. Builders and laborers "between jobs" worked alongside apprentices who needed experience, while interior furnishings and decorations were sourced locally from artists and community groups.

The school's alternative approach to education meant students had a chance to work part-time at the school cafeteria and bakery, selling products like muffins and bread rolls to the public. In addition to regular teachers, visiting artists, designers, and musicians ran workshops and gave demonstrations. Students themselves went on exchange to other countries. Gibson High didn't feel like a typical school, and it was for this reason Alana had chosen it. The school's board prided itself on its unconventional approach, but their desire to be at the forefront of change also led to some questionable decision-making. The school's librarian, for example, distrusted the Dewey System of classification, used in libraries the world over. She knew where every book was, however, and had an almost supernatural ability to detect when a book was out of place. In this way, Mrs. Heller made herself indispensable to the school … since she was the only one who knew where anything was. She was also very good at saying, "Shhhh!"

Alana and her friends were welcomed by the school's deputy principal, Mr. Turner – the head principal being strangely unavailable for the first day of term. "Gibson High's school motto," the moustached man intoned, "is '*A posse ad esse,*' which, for the Latin scholars among you, means, 'From possibility to actuality'. This is what we at the school wish for you all. May the gamut of experiences you have over the next six years with us exploit your potential to the full." Mr. Turner beamed – a rotund, Santa-like figure with rosy cheeks and a twinkle in his eye. Even the scattering of dandruff on his shoulders lent an illusion of snow. "So, Year Seven," he commanded, "explore, experiment, and enjoy!"

Maddie, Sofia, Alana and Khalilah exchanged delighted glances. "Exciting!" Sofia chirped.

Alana's first class for the day was physical education. Students used the gym, basketball court, and boxing ring of the Police Boys' Club next door. An evaluation exercise would assess their fitness levels and sport aptitude. Alana, Sofia, Maddie and Khalilah followed the other girls to change into their P.E. outfits.

"I'm looking forward to kickboxing," said

Maddie. "My cousins say it's a lot of fun."

"I hope we get to play soccer," said Alana.

"Me too," agreed Khalilah, a big soccer fan.

"Will we get to play soccer?" Sofia asked, consulting her Magic 8 Ball. "Hmm, it says *Probably*."

"How about kickboxing?" asked Maddie, peering over Sofia's shoulder while others looked on.

The Magic 8 Ball was adamant.

Absolutely not.

The small knot of students laughed.

Suddenly, a voice rang out, causing them to scatter, "Right, girls, you were supposed to be out of here three minutes ago. What's taking you so long?"

What the girls saw was a boy no taller than themselves. A sports cap shadowed a face of delicate features. Although he had a whistle and stopwatch around his neck, he looked far too young to be their teacher. Whoever he was, he was not happy to be kept waiting. Sofia, herself angry to be interrupted in a state of undress, exclaimed,

"What the heck, bird brain! You shouldn't even be in here," as she struggled to cover up. Sofia felt her privacy was always being invaded: her brothers at home often opened doors without knocking, and laughed at her attempts at modesty.

We've seen you in your undies before, they scoffed, or *As if we'd want to look anyway.*

The boy removed his sunglasses, taking in Sofia's purple hair, good luck charms, and *Hello Kitty* boypants. It was obvious he was less than impressed with what he saw. He looked around at the group.

"Thanks to your friend, here," he announced with a nod in Sofia's direction, "you have sixty seconds to get out for a warm-up lap around the gym. For every minute you're late, the number of laps doubles. I'm assuming you know how to count. Oh, and make sure all your jewelry is left in the changing room," he said with a sharp glance at Sofia. "You're not here to impress the boys."

That was their P.E. teacher?!

This was not *fantastique*, said Alana silently to herself. Not *fantastique* at all.

Everybody scrambled to finish dressing. Feet got tangled in neck holes, and T-shirts remained stubbornly inside out. The girls *whooshed* out of the changing room in a state of confusion. Nobody wanted to do extra laps if they could help it. Several of them shot Sofia a dark look before they left. Sofia looked for a locker, but there was nothing but benches and pigeon holes. She hid her charm bracelet, necklaces, and mood ring in her uniform, but not before asking her Magic 8 Ball a final question:

"Am I going to hate P.E.?"

Highly likely, it said before she rushed out to join the others.

Ten minutes later, the teacher addressed the students, most of who were puffing and wheezing from the extra laps. "Welcome to Gibson High School and the Police Boys' Club. My name is *Ms.* Kusmuk." The *Ms.* buzzed like a swarm of angry bees. "You can call me Coach."

The students shifted uncomfortably. Sofia was not the only one to assume their teacher was a male and a student, but she had a sneaky feeling she was the only one in the history of Gibson High to ever call the coach a bird brain.

"Ms. Coach Kusmuk, will we get to play soccer?" asked a boy Alana didn't know. His voice broke midway, starting out high, and then cracking into wobbly, deeper tone at the end, like a slippery dip. Some students gave a nervous giggle.

"Yes, at some point you will be. And it's "Coach" or "Ms Kusmuk," not both," she said, correcting him.

The boy's face, already flaming from his sing-song voice, turned an even brighter red.

"How about kickboxing?" came another question, this time from the back of the group.

"Definitely not. That's strictly for the Police Boys' Club and their teenage delinquents. Sorry," she smirked, not looking at all contrite, "the politically-correct term is 'Second-Chancers,'

I believe. Although, who knows," she said, her gaze finding Sofia's, "you could find yourselves part of their program."

When the coach finally shifted her gaze elsewhere, Sofia said to Alana in an undertone others could still hear, "See, I told you. The Magic 8 Ball never lies."

The next hour was harsh. They discovered muscles they didn't know they had, and learned to dread the sound of the whistle. *Peep peep* it would shrill as Coach Kusmuk bawled at them from the sidelines of the obstacle course. With a *Hup, hup, hup* and a *Come on, you can lift your legs higher,* she pushed them harder than a drill sergeant. One girl even rushed to the changing rooms to be sick.

Alana gave an encouraging smile to Khalilah, who struggled to keep up. Every so often, students stopped to have their heart rate tested and recorded. They were relieved when the coach stopped to take a phone call, but not before asking Sofia for a demonstration of squat jumps, which the others had to count. By the time they hit the showers, many of them were complaining of aches and pains.

Sofia was even more dismayed to discover her charm bracelet was gone!

"Perhaps it dropped when you got changed?"

"No. I was really careful to hide it in my uniform with the other stuff. See," she said holding out the rest of her jewelry, "they're still here."

Nothing could console Sofia, who valued the Magic 8 Ball more highly than any of the other charms. How would she decide things now?

"Who could have taken it?"

"Who would want to?"

But they were running late for their next class. The mystery of the missing charm bracelet would have to wait.

Alana put an arm around her friend. "Don't worry, Sofia. I'll find out who did this."

But Sofia didn't care who had done it. She just wanted her Magic 8 Ball charm back.

CHAPTER 6

Digital challenge.

Alana's second class was Information, Communication, and Technology, otherwise known as ICT. Their teacher, Mr. Boyd, was a lean man with a thin face and a nose that turned up at the tip. His habit of stroking his beard, which was a bright ginger color, lent him the air of a constantly grooming squirrel, which was reinforced by his scurried movements as he hopped from one desktop to another. Their first topic was social networks, he informed them. They would not only design and create one for use within the classroom, but also debate the pros and cons of social networking sites. This would allow them to discuss cyberbullying.

The four girls, along with their classmates, attacked the subject matter with enthusiasm. Maddie used social networking sites to connect with other musicians. They shared song ideas, wrote lyrics together and enjoyed jam sessions online. Some students described their experiences of gaming. They liked to role-play characters in fight games or quests, taking on identities very different to their own. Alana, a budding photographer, was a member of a social website for shared photos. She found the site inspirational as well as practical. Members provided technical tips on how to use cameras, improve photo composition, and gave advice on manipulating images.

At this point Khalilah jumped in. She had once been a victim of a practical joke: someone had changed her photo to make her look like a boy.

For Sofia, this spelled Social Death. "What did you do?" she gasped.

"I pretended the person in the photo was my twin brother, Abdul. 'Abdul' sent many embarrassing letters to the joker declaring his love. I was never bothered again."

"*Do* you have a twin?" Maddie asked.

"Not at all!"

The class laughed and gave Khalilah openly

admiring looks. Maddie, Alana and Sofia gazed at their new friend with greater respect. This was a girl who was not afraid to speak her mind, or twist situations to her advantage.

"That's a very creative approach to dealing with the bully, Khalilah. Well done. But often cyberbullying is anonymous. You don't know who the bully is," said Mr. Boyd, squinting at the class.

The conversation moved to ways in which bullying could be turned around when the identity of the bully was unknown – how the power could be shifted so the victim felt in control.

"I'm looking forward to listening to your ideas and using them in the social networking site we'll be setting up," Mr. Boyd explained to the students as they made to leave. "And as a fun exercise, try digitally reworking a photo of yourself. We'll put them up next week and play a game of 'Guess Who.' Make sure you get to know each other well, so you're not reliant on the image."

The students walked out, eagerly discussing their ideas. It seemed Sofia was the only one not looking forward to the task, until it was explained that she could digitally *enhance* her photo if she chose. The spring in Sofia's step returned. Now she could see what difference a nose job would make *before* she saved up to get one.

CHAPTER 7

When Life hands you an Opportunity, put on your... Rollerblades?

While the girls were experiencing their first day at high school, Emma was ordered to the salon. Eyebrows, underarms, and legs needed waxing, and a haircut was long overdue. Although nail art would have been nice, a manicure and pedicure took priority, and as Ling Ling reminded her, they could not perform miracles.

The Beauty Bar had been converted from a dingy, dark nightclub to a light, airy space that offered complete makeovers. Katriona and Ling Ling's two-bedroom flat sat above their makeover salon affording them views the length of King Street. Wedged between The Buff Barn – the bodybuilders' hang – and The Cuppa – a café for *serious* coffee fiends – a visit to the salon always sent Emma's nose into a headspin. Freshly ground beans dueled with the smell of sweat and fake tans. Up ahead, Emma spotted tendrils of smoke from the incense sticks of Inner Harmony winding their way toward her. With a quick wave to George and his long-time partner, William, who were taking their Boxer, Daisy, for a walk, Emma locked her car and rushed inside, bolting the door before the sickly sweet smell made her sick. It was always the same after holing up in her study for weeks on end with the computer. Emma responded to fresh air and sunlight with all the enthusiasm of a vampire.

"So what can you tell me about Slam Guru?" Emma said, trying not to flinch as strips of wax were ripped from her body.

"He's 6 foot 3, has an in-cre-di-ble body, is 32, still single and …"

"Katriona! This is work!"

"I'm just saying he's available. And you're still young and not in bad shape … considering you do zero exercise. After two hours here, you'll be looking gorgeous and …"

"All work and no play makes Emma a dull girl," Ling Ling interrupted with a knowing nod.

Emma ignored the hint and tried to keep track of Katriona's prattle about the rock star, but it was difficult. Somehow, Katriona knew what his regular takeout restaurant was, what day he was born, what weight he bench-pressed and his favorite color, but Emma could use none of this information for the interview. The lecture became a blur. Slam Guru trivia merged with what Katriona was feeding her pet cat Jinx, who apparently was off his food.

Emma came back to earth with a bump as the final rebellious hairs were yanked from her eyebrows.

"Owww!"

"Too long, Emma. I keep telling you. You leave it too long, it hurts more. Don't wait so long."

It was obvious Ling Ling was referring to more than Emma's erratic trips to the salon. A look of panic entered Emma's eyes. For the past few months, her friends had hinted she should consider dating. But how could she? Years ago, Emma had met the love of her life and never looked back. Hugo had known her inside out, lived with every disgusting habit, seen her at her worst, and *still* loved her. He was her rock. He was her world. He was gone …

"*Da dah*!" Ling Ling spun Emma around to reveal her new look. It included a short, chic haircut, sleek eyebrows and skin that glowed. Katriona and Ling Ling looked very proud.

"Your clothes are over there, Em. Just pop them on, then we'll do a final touch-up."

"Thank you!"

With the new dress halfway over her head, Emma called for the time. Her question met a wall of silence – the kind of silence that comes when people hold their breath.

"Ummm, don't be mad, okay? But it's 10:15."

"What?!"

Emma shuffled out from behind the screen, the dress still twisted around her upper torso. "It can't be 10:15. I've been watching your clock. Look. It only says 9:45."

"Oh, that's the time in Adelaide. *This* is the time in Sydney," Ling Ling said, showing Emma her bubble watch, which now read 10:16. There was no way she would make it to The Waterfront Café by 10:30, especially with King Street's notorious traffic.

With a scream of frustration, Emma ranted about being late, being killed by James, and then being fined when she saw the wheel clamp on her car, parked outside. She was close to tears when Katriona slammed a pair of Rollerblades onto the bench. A look of horror crossed Emma's face. What was her friend suggesting?

"Katriona, I haven't done this since I was a kid. Plus, there's no way I'll be able to make it. I'll call James to reschedule or something."

"You are not canceling on The Guru. Nobody cancels on The Guru. Or reschedules. This is a Once-In-A-Lifetime-Opportunity, so suck it up, and get them on!"

Emma whimpered as she squeezed her feet into

the sparkly Rollerblades, half a size too small. Her memories of rollerblading were not good. She was sure it had involved a trip to the hospital, and at least one broken bone. Emma wobbled as she made it to her feet and clumped to the front door.

"Bon voyage," Katriona said, giving Emma a vigorous push to get her started. They listened to a strangled wail as Emma glided away down the road.

"You know I always liked the back of that dress better than the front. That was a good idea to put it behind," said Ling Ling, as she continued to wave.

Katriona looked in dismay at the mistake. The dress *was* on the wrong way! She thought of yelling a warning, but what was the point? They would only get into trouble again. If they were lucky, Slam Guru would be so distracted by Emma's gorgeous hair that he wouldn't notice.

The wheels in Katriona's mind continued to turn as she drew a second conclusion. Emma, her best friend, was off to meet Slam Guru, her favorite rock star Of All Time.

In.

The.

Flesh.

What was she waiting here for?

Katriona exchanged her own shoes for a pair of Rollerblades. Then she threw another pair of blades at Ling Ling, urging her to do the same. They were going to follow Emma to her interview so Slam Guru could meet the woman of his dreams … Katriona!

CHAPTER 8

S.O.S. ... Skating, Old men, and Stalkers.

It was a typical Monday morning and Newtown was as busy as ever – cafés that opened for breakfast served "coffees-to-go," young families walked to daycare, while buskers made use of summer's last days to try their luck with commuters. Those that sang had to compete with the deafening sounds of planes flying above, the thundering arterial traffic on Newtown's main road, King Street, and the constant rumble of trains below. Emma clung to the pedestrian crossing sign for balance. The Rollerblades were pinching her toes, and her thigh muscles were already protesting. That said, even though the roads were bumper to bumper with cars, she was halfway to her destination and only five minutes had passed. It looked like she was going to make it after all … as long as she didn't trip.

The light turned green. Emma pushed off and lurched forward. She passed the University of Sydney with its impressive gates and sandstone walls, hoping her bizarre combination of Rollerblades and LBD (Little Black Dress) did not look too out of place. She took comfort in the fact that many people these days (especially students) were cycling, skateboarding, and rollerblading, to be more environmentally friendly. Emma turned her gaze from the imposing buildings just in time to narrowly miss a mother and her stroller, and a couple of young professionals running for the bus.

Emma shifted the strap of her bag to help regain her balance. She hugged it close to her side as the wind whipped at her hair. There was no way she was going to lose this bag. It was too important. She'd seen it while shopping at Glebe Markets with Ling Ling and it had been love at first sight. Each section of fabric looked like it had been lovingly chosen before being pieced together into the perfect combination.

Glass beads and tiny circles of mirror were sewn into the fabric, in turn reflecting fringe trims and catching the light. Plus the bag was huge. Emma liked a bag that could fit in all the stuff she packed for emergencies.

The canny stall-holder had noticed the glaze over Emma's eyes. "Feel how soft it is." Emma obediently stroked the bag as if it were a Persian cat. "You won't find any bag the same. The fabrics are hand-dyed. Some of them vintage. Each one is unique." Emma eyed the colors appreciatively. "And look," he said, holding the bag open, "you could fit my mother-in-law in there and never find her again." He laughed. "On second thoughts, I think I'll keep it for myself."

Emma reached for the bag in a panic as he pretended to put it under the table, but Ling Ling held out a warning hand.

"How much?" Ling Ling demanded.

"In the shops, this sells for $450, but," he tapped fingertip to nose, leaned in so close they could smell the coffee on his breath, "for today

only, I'm selling it for $300."

"Why so expensive one? Cannot be, lah," Ling Ling scoffed. "Don't cheat me, 'kay? Fifty, lah. I give you fifty." Ling Ling said, slipping into Singapore slang as she engaged in her second favorite pastime – shopping! Her favorite pastime was eating ... of course.

"Fifty? Oh no, no, no. Fifty is a ridiculous price. I could come down to $280. That's it."

Ling Ling shooed the man's offer away like an annoying fly. "Eh, Uncle, I no tourist one. I know you up the price three times. Okay, last price – $70!"

The stall-holder grabbed his heart as if in sudden pain. "Stop it! You're killing me. $250. That's my final offer."

Ling Ling remained unsatisfied. "Don't con me, lah, Uncle! This price I can get hundred of this in China." Ling Ling tossed the bag onto the table with disdain.

The man's eyes turned steely. "$200. Take it. Or leave it."

Emma reached for her wallet, but was stopped by Ling Ling a second time. "Okay, neh-mind. Bye," and with a jaunty wave, Ling Ling dragged Emma to another stall, furtively whispering, "Pretend you're looking at something else. Any minute now he'll come chasing us with an offer of a hundred."

But the stall-holder did not come chasing. When they returned – casually, of course – he took great satisfaction in telling them it had been sold. Nothing Ling Ling said could console Emma. That same afternoon, Emma's mother – who lived an hour away – dropped by and handed her daughter a bag. *The* bag. It was even more beautiful than she'd remembered.

"I found this at the markets," Emma's mother said, hands on hips. "After I told him I'd come *all the way* from Campbelltown I got the man down from $300 to $50!" she crowed, securing Ling Ling's unswerving devotion and veneration forever.

Emma was brought back from her pleasant

daydream with a jerk. She looked down and realized the strap of her precious bag was caught. She couldn't imagine how it had happened. One minute she was rollerblading with her bag held securely to her side, the next minute her bag was snagged on the handle of an old person's electric wheelchair. At first Emma pretended it was a coincidence that she was rollerblading next to him – all the while trying to untangle her bag. Even when she knew her persistent presence and nearness was making the elderly man nervous, she smiled and held on. But every attempt to unhook the strap failed. The bag refused to budge. The first time he glanced over his shoulder at Emma, he gave her a slight smile full of curiosity. The second time was less friendly, and by the third, he was convinced she had evil intentions.

"Help!" he cried, clutching his plastic bag of adult diapers. "This woman is trying to rob me. Help me, somebody!"

"No. No, I'm not. Please. I'm sorry. Terribly sorry. My bag ..." Emma tried to explain, but passersby were quick to come to the old man's defense, heedless of her excuses.

The man's wheelchair surged forward in an effort to shake Emma off. Well-meaning citizens jogged alongside to pry Emma's grip from her bag. Emma's legs crisscrossed and wobbled as she was dragged onward, under attack. They looked like a massive conga line, zig zagging all over the pavement. Suddenly, a wet stream of pigeon poo fell from the sky, which the old man reacted to with surprising speed. With a sharp turn and screech of wheels, Emma's bag became unhooked. She was free at last. The old man spun round and shook an angry fist, yelling "Hooligan!" before disappearing in a cloud of dust.

The substantial crowd, likewise, tutted and wagged their fingers with disapproval.

"You should be ashamed of yourself," she heard them mutter as they went their separate ways.

A city clock gave a short chime to indicate the half-hour. 10:30. James was going to kill her!

Emma put her head down, secured her bag for

a second time and pumped her arms like a speed skater. She refused to miss this career opportunity because of a paranoid pensioner. The gentle slope gave her the boost she needed. The breeze rippled her dress. Chinatown was up ahead. If she squinted, she could almost see the glint of water that was Darling Harbor. If she had been a real estate agent, she most definitely would have.

Emma arrived at the entrance of The Waterfront Café in a cloud of burnt rubber. Beads of sweat lined her forehead, and her arms and neck glowed. James was pacing out the front. He looked ready to explode. He cut Emma's explanation short and told her the best news of the whole morning: Slam Guru had sent his apologies. He was running late and would be there as soon as he could. The extra time allowed Emma not only to catch her breath, but also to read the biography James had prepared for the interview … just in case.

"I figured Katriona's information may not be very helpful. Nice haircut, by the way." James's teeth flashed as he began to relax. He did a double-take of her outfit, began to say something, but changed his mind with a dismissive wave of his hand. There was no time for Emma to change and the dress didn't look *that* odd, back-to-front. He motioned her to hurry and get started on the research.

By the time Slam Guru arrived, looking suave and powerful in a casual T-shirt and jeans, Emma was feeling equally cool and collected. The only thing making her feel uncomfortable was the fit of her dress, which sat awkwardly on her shoulders. Emma shoved her concerns aside. She was the first to admit she was clueless about fashion.

Katriona had not been exaggerating – Slam Guru was every inch the powerful, charismatic rock star, Emma concluded, as she took his hand in a firm handshake. Emma glanced down and noticed that Slam's skin color – that of a strong espresso – showed up in stark contrast to her own. A Celtic tattoo stretched up the length of one arm: one of no less than fifteen, according to Katriona.

His dark head of hair was cut fashionably close to his scalp with sideburns that flowed into a stylised shadow of a beard that looked hand-drawn. The beard's point finished under his full, bottom lip like the tip of a dragon's tail. Emma knew that beneath his sunglasses, Slam's eyes were blue, although she wondered cynically if they really were as vivid as the posters made them out to be. She'd worked with James long enough to know that you could accentuate anyone's eye color with a click of a button. Almost as if he could read her mind, the rocker pushed his sunglasses up onto his head and flashed a smile that made Emma's heart falter. Those eyes were lethal. The posters didn't even come close. Emma shoved her stuttering alter ego aside to assume a self-assured air. She was a professional and she had a job to do.

The view from the upper level of the café was spectacular, a detail Slam Guru was quick to comment on. This led them to chat with ease about travel and favorite cities, drifting from topic to topic while James took discrete shots. Slam

Guru's voice was deep, measured, and calm. His laughter, when it came, was throaty and musical. Emma was ecstatic. The interview was going to be a breeze. She leaned forward to switch on her recorder while Slam Guru adjusted his sunglasses against the sudden glare of the sun.

"Slam Guru, you're at the zenith of your career. Did you ever imagine you would reach such a high level of success growing up in the slums of Chicago?"

"No."

Emma paused, waiting for Slam Guru to give more detail. When none was forthcoming, she pressed on.

"It must have been incredibly challenging with violence and drugs on your doorstep. How did you manage to steer clear of it?"

"You do what you have to do," he responded in a deep voice.

Again, Emma waited for more information. Again, Slam Guru was silent. The rocker shifted in his seat and fiddled with his sunglasses. It was impossible to guess what he was thinking. Whether he realized it or not, Slam Guru's body was rigid. The rest of his responses to Emma's questions were equally stiff and awkward. In frustration, she switched the recorder off. Slam Guru and Emma returned to chatting easily about his forthcoming tour.

Emma waited until the waiter finished refilling their glasses with water before switching the recorder back on. She sensed, rather than saw, Slam Guru's body tense again. The recording was obviously making him feel self-conscious. If Emma was to make it through the interview with something printable, she had to put him at ease. In desperation, she changed tack, dredging up the mountain of Guru-trivia Katriona had dumped in her brain.

"So you were born on a Tuesday."

"I don't know. I've heard someone tell me I was." *Silence.*

"A little bird told me your favorite takeout is chili-fried chicken from *Chicks 'N Stix*."

"Yeah it is." *More silence.*

"You obviously work out a lot. You're up to bench-pressing, what, 150 kilos or something?"

"I am."

"And you like to use *Scents of the Sea* bubble bath?"

"I do."

"Is it true you've got a birthmark on your …"

But Slam Guru did not allow her to finish. He gave Emma a look filled with distrust.

"How do you know all this stuff? It's the kind of information that stalker, Katalina, or whatever her name was, found out about me."

Emma pounced on the first piece of information Slam Guru had volunteered. "Do you have a lot of trouble with stalkers?"

"Not really. My fans respect my privacy, but her? She's a complete nut job. One *scary* woman. My security guards found her rifling through trash in my London house. She even broke in and used my spa! There were bubbles all over the place. It got so bad I had to take out a restraining order against her."

A chill traveled the length of Emma's spine. Suddenly all the pieces fell into place. She remembered reading about an unidentified woman invading Slam Guru's privacy. The woman had followed him everywhere, sent him fan mail every day, and sat outside his home just to catch a glimpse. One day, she broke into his home, and was found in his living room sharing doughnuts with his prized fish. The woman's camera revealed she had taken photos of herself in each of his rooms, posing in Slam Guru's own bathrobe. The incident coincided with an increase in Slam Guru's security, Katriona's trip to England, and her unexpected delay in the country's capital …

"A restraining order? As in, she wasn't allowed within a hundred meters of you?" Emma inquired weakly.

"Twenty. If she gets within twenty meters of me, she gets hauled to jail. The woman is crazy. No sense of boundaries," Slam Guru shuddered. "I've got bodyguards for my bodyguards because of her."

Then suddenly, like a scene from a nightmare, a leg flopped over the side of the balcony. Fire-engine red toenail polish glinted in Sydney's morning sun.

It was Katriona.

CHAPTER 9

Intense. Insane. Same-same lah!

"Yoo hooooo! Slam Guuuu-ruuuu! It's me. Katriona. Remember, we met in London?" Katriona's head popped over the top of the balcony to join her leg. An arm followed. She looked like the disembodied work of a magician. Katriona attempted a casual smile, as if climbing up to a first-floor balcony to grab a coffee was something she did every day.

Slam Guru's chair crashed to the floor as he moved with uncommon speed. "You?" he yelled, pointing a finger. "How did you find me? What are you doing here?"

"I just thought I'd pop over and say hi. You know, welcome you to Sydney. I mean, we didn't get to talk much last time. I think we got off on the wrong foot ..."

"You broke into my home. You had a bubble bath in my spa. You wore my bathrobe!" With each accusation, Slam Guru's normally rich, deep voice rose an octave. Any higher and he would sound like a chipmunk.

"You remembered," Katriona sighed, eyes shiny with emotion as she clutched her chest … and then fell.

"Katriona!" Emma unfroze as she rushed to save her friend. But she needn't have worried: Katriona had fallen from the first floor on to Ling Ling, who was on her way up. Their combined fall was cushioned by the shade sails of the café below.

"You … you know this woman?" The note of betrayal and panic in Slam Guru's voice was obvious.

Emma turned around and gave a feeble smile. "Kind of. She's a nice person once you get to know her. Just a little … intense."

"She's not intense, she's *insane*! This interview is over. Security!"

Within seconds, Slam Guru's bodyguards formed a human barrier. They ushered him back to his hotel.

"Well, that has to be the shortest interview in history," Emma said with a forlorn look. "I'm so sorry, James. I've really messed up this time."

"Don't worry. I'll see what I can do to salvage something from this mess. Once he's had time to calm down, I'm sure he'll be fine."

The *clunk, clunk, clunk* of high-heeled wedges announced the arrival of a disheveled Katriona and a rather bruised Ling Ling, Rollerblades slung over their shoulders.

"Where is he? Where did he go?"

James didn't bother to berate Emma's friend about missed opportunities, or point out that, because of her, Slam Guru had run from the café, all but screaming.

"He had to rush off, Katriona. I'm sorry. I know you wanted to talk, but he's a busy man. You know how it is."

Katriona straightened her outfit as she flicked back her blonde hair and leered at him.

"It's okay. Slam remembered me in his bathrobe. It's obvious he can't get an image like that out of his mind. Maybe we should shoot some shots of our own?" Katriona said, bumping James playfully with her hip.

James picked himself up off the floor and backed away with lightning speed. "Sorry, Katriona, but I'm also very busy. Very, very busy," he yelped, before grabbing his camera equipment and charging from the room.

CHAPTER 10

It's a mystery.

Alana, Sofia, Maddie and Khalilah spread out all over Alana's living room, to do the first day's homework. Alana's house as a base was a no-brainer. Even without the drone of planes skimming the rooftops, it was still quieter than Sofia's house and her noisy brothers. Maddie's younger siblings would have pestered them to play. Khalilah's mom was working on her PhD, and had her own pile of books and papers strewn everywhere. Before long, conversation drifted to the mystery of the missing charm bracelet.

"We need to go through our suspects and establish motive and opportunity," said Alana, who was a big fan of "whodunits." She drew up two columns: "Who would *want* to do it" and "Who *could* have done it."

"Some of the girls were pretty annoyed at me for having to do extra laps," said Sofia.

"But everybody was in the gym the whole time," Khalilah chipped in.

Alana, who was good at noticing things, disagreed. "No. Remember there was that girl who got sick and went back to the changing rooms?" They tried to picture what the girl looked like, and who she was.

"Laura, or Lorna, or something?"

"I'm sure she joined a couple of juggling workshops at the Community Center," Alana said, looking at Maddie who shook her head. Laura-or-Lorna wasn't someone she could recall. "Don't you remember? She was that shy girl. Always took ages to decide what to order at the Milk Bar."

Finally, Maddie nodded her head. She remembered the lunchtime lines very well. And it was always the same girl, *umming* and *ahhing* about what snack to buy – apple or banana – or which hot meal.

"Although Coach Kusmuk left, too. Wanting revenge for being mistaken for a boy would be a strong motive."

"And being called a bird brain."

"Well, she *was* very unsympathetic when I told her," said Sofia uncertainly, recalling the way Coach Kusmuk's eyes had lit up. She twisted her mood ring nervously, now a murky brown.

"But why take only the charm bracelet? Why not take everything?"

"Maybe she knew it was a *lucky* Magic 8 Ball. I mean, sure, you can buy these things off the internet, but mine is the Real Deal," she replied, now subconsciously rubbing the rounded belly of a Buddha pendant.

Maddie looked skeptically at Sofia's bracelet of four leafed-clover, three-legged toad, and rabbit's foot. Sofia claimed each one was Lucky. Each one was the Real Deal. *Not very lucky for the rabbit*, she thought to herself.

"Hmmm, it *is* a mystery," said Alana, as she made notes in her notebook. "The first thing to do, I suppose, is check out this Laura or Lorna person, and Coach Kusmuk for any Suspicious

Behavior."

The girls digested this in silence as they tried to figure out what Suspicious Behavior might entail.

"Whoever took it is probably as superstitious as I am," said Sofia. "If we can catch them consulting the Magic 8 Ball before making a decision, then we've solved the mystery."

"Let's just see if either of them is superstitious first. I doubt they'd openly use something stolen." Alana saw her friend's crestfallen face. "Trust me, Sofia," she told her friend. "We'll find it. I promise."

Slightly cheered, the girls turned their attention back to their homework.

By the time Emma and her friends arrived home after some retail therapy of the shop-'til-you-drop-kind, the girls had moved on to their ICT project. There were photos of themselves on the laptop screen, alongside digitally-altered versions which they adjusted.

"Hey, look what happens when I do this,"

Alana chortled, as with a swipe of her fingers on the screen her forehead blew up, making her look like a caveman. The three girls rolled around laughing, and then tried to outdo her by making modifications of their own.

Maddie transformed herself into an *anime*-looking character with over-sized eyes and a head full of curls. Sofia chose to give herself enormous pointy ears, blue skin, and flappy jowels, while Khalilah's head sprouted a mohawk, bulbous eyes, and puffy lips.

"I look so boodiful," she said, imitating her photo with puckered mouth.

"Well if you ask me, I think it's a huge improvement," Katriona said with a sniff. Alana and her friends ignored her.

Alana's mom walked in, parading a "new" hat from the local thrift store, a Mexican *sombrero* so big it flopped over her eyes and most of her face. As she twirled, the tassles flew about in a blur of color. Katriona and Ling Ling egged her on with a drumbeat. They clapped and stamped their feet, shaking the living room with cries of *Arriba!* and *Andale!*

"Nice outfit, Mrs. Oakley, but why are you wearing it back-to-front?" Sofia said. She held up her magazine to show Emma the very dress she was wearing, on the cover.

Emma tilted back her hat, clenched her fists and rounded on her two friends, who were now edging toward the doorway.

"Katriona, Ling Ling, how could you? Oh, how embarrassing! On top of everything else?!" she sputtered as words failed her.

"It's okay, Emma. Maybe if you do the interview again, you can wear the dress the right way round, and he will not recognize you," suggested Ling Ling.

"I'll be lucky if he doesn't slap a restraining order on me, too. What were you thinking, Katriona? Breaking and entering? A bubble bath? His bathrobe? No wonder he felt grossed out."

Alana interrupted her mom with a cuddle from behind as she began a monologue:

"Hi, Alana. How was your first day of school? What are you up to? A new school project? Oh and look, there's Maddie and Sofia. And a new girl. Where's my manners? Hi, I'm …"

Emma had the grace to look ashamed. "It's okay, I've got it from here, Alana. I'm so sorry, girls," said Emma, turning to address the three youths, who were waiting with huge grins on their faces. "Let's try this again, shall we? Hi, I'm Emma. Lovely to meet you …?"

"Khalilah."

"Khalilah. Hey Maddie, Sofia. You girls are shooting up so fast I'll have to buy higher heels to keep up! Did you all have a good summer? Can I get you anything to eat?"

"I was wondering if they could stay for dinner? We've got a project, and we'd like to have it sorted by this week." Emma's eyes widened in panic, the trauma of burnt pots a fresh memory. "Don't worry," Alana quickly continued, "I've organized pasta. You won't have to cook."

Khalilah broke into the conversation with an

apologetic look. "I'm sorry, Alana. I cannot stay for dinner. I'm not allowed to eat anything that isn't *halal*. My religion forbids it."

"That's okay. Mom is vegetarian and I don't cook any meat at home."

Maddie gave Khalilah a curious look. "Are you vegetarian too? Is that what *halal* means?"

"No. I can eat meat but the animal needs to be slaughtered in a special way and with a prayer. But of course there are some things which are strictly forbidden, like pork, which we Muslims cannot eat at all."

"What? No bacon, no pepperoni pizza?" cried Sofia, aghast.

"No," said Khalilah with a smile. It was clear she was used to explaining her eating habits.

"So how come you're vegetarian, Mrs. Oakley?" asked Sofia. She couldn't imagine her carnivorous brothers living without meat. It was a choice Emma's own mother had difficulty understanding.

"Meat? What's wrong with meat? People back home in the Philippines would kill for such luxuries!" she'd cry. But Emma could not be persuaded to take the plate from her mother. It was all she could do not to run from the roasting animal, rotating round and round over hot coals, apple nestled neatly in its mouth.

Emma curled up on the sofa to massage her feet, sore from the tight-fitting Rollerblades and subsequent shopping marathon. "Well, to cut a long story short, I was researching an article on chicken farming, and I felt so sorry for those poor, cooped-up animals with clipped wings, I decided to give it up."

"You forgot to mention that you and your two buddies over there staged a raid and got caught 'liberating' a truck full of poultry," said Alana, using her hands to mime the quotation marks for "liberating."

Emma gave the girls a weak grin as a memory of pink ski masks flashed through her mind.

"Or that you used Auntie Katriona's pet cat, Jinx, to round them up."

"Who knew a three-legged cat could move so

fast?" Emma muttered.

"Or that I had to bail you out of jail."

By this stage, Alana was looming over Emma, one foot tapping while Emma's petite frame burrowed further into the cushions.

"Well, anyway. If my decision to become a vegetarian has saved even one life, then it's all been worthwhile."

If Khalilah was unsure about her new friend and family before, she was not now. Although Alana and Emma were clearly two people as different from each other as was possible, their hearts were definitely in the right place. She bit her top lip to stop herself from grinning. Maddie and Sofia also struggled to keep a straight face: they already knew life with Alana and Mrs. Oakley was never boring.

"It looks like I'm staying for dinner, then," Khalilah said with a smile. "Let me call home to make sure it's okay."

CHAPTER 11

A seed is sown.

Since dinner was taken care of, Emma ducked into her office to continue her research. The interview with Slam Guru had not gone well, but she had a hunch she was keen to pursue. Within minutes, her back took on the familiar stoop of an organist seated at a Gothic organ as she punched her computer keys. She was fully engrossed in her work. Nothing short of an earthquake would move her for hours.

In utter fascination, Katriona and Ling Ling watched the four girls work on their project. Since when was homework so much fun? In Russia, where Katriona had grown up, she had frightening memories of teachers with stubble and bad breath, pacing the floor with a cane that found its mark should you be unlucky enough to provide the wrong answer. The male teachers were even worse! For Ling Ling it was equally confusing: school had meant hours of memorization and repetition. There were approximately 50,000 characters in the Chinese language, and you needed to know at least 5,000 just to read a newspaper! Her family in Singapore was bitterly disappointed to discover she had no ambition to be an accountant and zero desire to join the family firm.

"But why not?" her father exclaimed after listening to her plans. "You're so gifted. Plus you're a Shu. Our name *means* 'number.' My father was an auditor. My father's father was an auditor. And his father before him. Impossible you should want to do anything else." He turned to his wife. "It must be *your* side of the family." His wife chose not to talk about her husband's brother, who had run away to study law. Nobody talked about him any more.

Ling Ling had been quite happy to move to Australia, where people valued a pretty set of nails just as much as a neatly solved equation. When Alana asked her why she should want to waste her time scrubbing and decorating people's feet, she replied, "People smile at you after you paint pretty flowers on their nails. Not so many after you tell them how much tax they owe." This did not mean Ling Ling shunned numbers altogether. Ling Ling's "gift" with digits and formulas always paid off at the stock market. But it was just a means to an end. The Beauty Bar she ran with Katriona was her true passion.

The studious silence of the room was broken by occasional snickers and snorts from the two adults. Ling Ling and Katriona, inspired by Alana's school assignment, played with an app on Ling Ling's phone. It morphed their photos so their features changed to drooping eyes, flattened noses, and spinning ears. After the fifth interruption, Alana could take no more.

"Do you mind?" she grumbled.

As soon as she returned to her work, Katriona placed her hand on her hip and mouthed, "Do you mind?" behind her back. This sent the two of them into another fit of laughter. Alana's answering glare contained the full force of a disgruntled librarian.

Ling Ling was the first to quiet down. She sidled up to Maddie.

"Whatcha doin'?" she said, one leg swinging over the arm of the couch.

Maddie gave Ling Ling a wary glance. She was not sure what to make of this woman who was so … pink.

"I'm checking different social networking sites. See, this one connects you to your friends, and then your friends' friends, and then *their* friends. It's quite a neat way to find people you haven't kept in touch with." She pointed to the next window on her screen. "This one puts you in touch with people you don't know, but who have a common interest."

At this piece of information, Ling Ling's leg paused mid-swing. She peered at the computer with newfound intensity.

"Ve-ry in-te-res-ting. Don't you think it is interesting, Katriona?" she said with a pointed glance.

Katriona, however, was inspecting her nails for chips, and missed Ling Ling's look of meaning.

"So you're saying that I, or Katriona if she wanted to, could connect with a complete stranger using this, this ... website, and it would match me up with the right person? A possible friend? Perhaps even the love of my life to go on dates with, and marry, and live happily ever after?" Ling Ling jumped up and down with Katriona, who now understood the source of her friend's excitement.

Maddie screwed up her face in disgust as she muttered, "I guess so."

Alana glanced up from her screen. "Sorry, Auntie Katriona. There's no website in the world which can help you with that one. Not unless you use someone else's photograph."

Katriona's answering glare changed to one of fiendish delight as another idea took hold.

This germ of an idea, starting out smaller than a microbe, took root in Ling Ling and Katriona's minds. It was an idea that grew ... and grew.

CHAPTER 12

The point of no return.

The dining room filled with the clink of glass, the clatter of cutlery, and the din of conversation as the girls ate and chatted. Emma took the opportunity to escape, and grabbed some pasta to eat on the go. But it was likely her food would grow cold and hard by the time she got around to it. She used to let forgotten bowls of congealed food pile up on books and papers until one day, fed up, Alana had placed every single dirty bowl and plate in a line, from her mom's study to the kitchen. It was like a trail on a three-dimensional map. Emma got the hint and, from then on, returned the dishes, and occasionally washed them, if she wasn't too immersed in work. From the frenetic *tap, tap, tap* of the computer keys, Emma's dinner, (for tonight anyway) would be cold pasta again.

In the next room, the four new high-schoolers were enjoying the second part of the assignment:

research for a game of Guess Who? Questions flew about the room with the energy of buzzing mosquitoes.

"Okay, how about pets? Anyone got one?"

"Do little brothers and sisters count?"

"Oh, don't be so mean, Maddie!" said Sofia. "I have one. He's a mongrel named Nostradamus – Mom let me rescue him from an animal shelter because the ad said he was 'on death's door' … that was six years ago. I don't think Mom and Dad expected him to last *this* long."

"I have a cat," volunteered Khalilah. "She's called Sushi. But she's so fat now, maybe I should call her Sumo." The girls laughed. "I got her as a present when we moved here from Brunei. How about you, Alana?"

"Oh no. No pets allowed here, are you kidding me? My mom is a disaster when it comes to animals," she said. Alana hadn't always lived in Marrickville in a (quite) big house, with a garden and do-up potential. She used to live in a flat in Newtown, very small (tiny really), with a shared courtyard decorated with broken cement urns and a small square of grass. It didn't take long before it was too small for the stray cats and dogs her mom collected with the same ease lint collected on clothes. Alana's dad, Hugo, rather than pointing out the impracticality of their "growing family" had simply announced that they'd be better off in a house. And so they'd moved and the menagerie with them, although not to the animals' advantage: The cats ran away. The guinea pig had a heart attack. The goat, called Guts, died after eating a football. The fish was a suspected suicide.

"But the worst was Choo Choo, my hamster," Alana said with a sad shake of her head.

"Poor Choo Choo," sympathized Maddie and Sofia, who had heard the story before.

"What happened?"

"One night, Mom left the cage door open, and of course he went exploring. A jogger saw him disappear up the exhaust pipe of the neighbor's Vespa. Mom tried to lure him out with food, but

I think he was so fat from her Little Treats, he got stuck."

"So what did she do?"

"She struck a match, hoping the light would attract him instead. Boy, was she wrong!" Alana shook her head. "The flame exploded because of the gas left in the pipe so that, *Boom!* Out shoots Choo Choo like a cannonball. Mom gets carted off to the burn unit and, well, I guess you could say Choo Choo had an unplanned cremation."

The girls digested this news in silence.

Katriona and Ling Ling, listening at the door, crept back to the computer. They typed the words "*animal lover*" into a blank space on the dating website, HookUp.

"Mom cried for a whole week, she felt so bad," they heard Alana continue. "I just couldn't get angry."

S-o-f-t-h-e-a-r-t-e-d, Katriona typed.

As the four girls shared information – from their favorite color to what music they listened to – Ling Ling and Katriona continued to fill out the form, which promised to find the most compatible male for Emma to date.

Katriona was stumped. "What shall we put down for interests?"

"We cannot write she is a workaholic. Too boring."

"Or shopping. Men will run a mile." Katriona paused. "She deserves someone fun. Why don't we put down rock climbing, hang gliding, and bungy jumping?" she asked, as she concentrated hard on the screen.

"But none of that is true."

"Well this isn't a true *photo* of her, either, but we have to start somewhere. Those looks won't last forever, and our salon can only do so much," she said, pressing *Enter*.

When people used to communicate the Old-Fashioned Way, with stamps and stuff, you wrote letters. If you changed your mind, the piece of paper could be torn up and thrown away. We live in different times now. We live in a digital age where you press *Send* and the message is sent.

Instantly. There is no paper to rip. No words to take back. No rewind or pause.

At the click of a button, Katriona placed all of them on a path from which nobody could return.

CHAPTER 13

Whenever you need a hole to swallow you up, it's never there!

It took two days of intense negotiations before Slam Guru agreed to a second meeting. In the early evening, under the bright lights of Sydney's Darling Harbor, James and Emma waited to see if the deal would come off.

"I used the last of my favors to reschedule this interview," James grumbled. "Not to mention getting exclusive use of the Sydney Aquarium at night. Thanks to your friends, I am now committed to shooting a calendar of Delores DeMontford and her poodles."

"You're the best, James. You know that?" said Emma, as she looped an arm through his.

"I'm a bit curious, though. Why do you want to do the interview here?"

A hint of a smile played at the corners of Emma's mouth. "Think about it. Slam Guru is in Sydney to

be the new face of 'H2O Heroes' – an organization
dedicated to saving aquatic environments and
sea life. He uses 'Scents of the Sea' bubble bath,
has a huge aquarium in his own home, and a pet
cockatoo called Jaws. I figure he *has* to be a bit
of an aquatic fan. Besides, Slam Guru was getting
spooked by my recorder the other day. I need him
to be completely relaxed if this is going to work."

James felt having a stalker couldn't have been
very relaxing, either. But since that stalker was one
of Emma's closest friends, he merely murmured,
"You'd better be right," before catching sight of the
rocker and his crew. This time, Slam was wearing
a leather jacket over a faded T-shirt and jeans. He
ran his fingers, which were covered in thick rings
fashioned into skulls, through the stubble of his
dark hair. Even though James couldn't see through
Slam's trademark sunglasses, he could sense the
musician's eyes glancing uneasily from side to side.
Slam Guru looked like the kind of man who could
easily play the hero in any Tough Guy flick – and
yet he twitched like an anxious rabbit.

The aquarium's manager opened the staff entrance. The group ghosted in. Before any of Slam's minders could stop him, the star-struck administrator grabbed his palm. He pumped it up and down and grinned like a maniac.

"It's an honor, an honor," he repeated, until Slam Guru managed to retrieve his hand. "If there's anything you need, anything at all, please do not hesitate to ask. I am completely at your disposal."

James escorted the man to his office, thanking him for accommodating his unusual request. This left Emma alone with Slam Guru and his bodyguards, who looked like they had doubled since last time. They looked about frequently and whispered to invisible colleagues on walkie-talkies.

Emma felt her stomach tighten as she took in a deep breath. She felt a sudden urge to run away.

"I wasn't going to come." Slam's voice was husky. "But then your choice of ... location changed my mind."

Emma breathed out and relaxed. Her hunch

was spot on. Everything was going to be fine. With renewed confidence, Emma led Slam Guru through the aquarium's walkways until they could hear the lyrical sounds of classical music weaving through the air. They came to a standstill at a massive glass wall reaching from floor to ceiling. Behind the meters-high wall were myriad colors, moving and flickering in the light. Hundreds of tropical fish swam in schools, darting in and out of rocks. Luminescent coral glowed. Larger pelagic fish slipped past with an elegant flick of the tail.

It was like standing on the bottom of the sea. The fish in the massive aquarium glided with ease, the grace of their movement heightened by the lilting notes of Debussy's "Claire de Lune" filling the room.

Nobody said a word. Even the bodyguards were spellbound.

"One of my favorite places," Emma said simply, motioning with a hand at the wall. She tried to place her arm around the musician's shoulders but, since he was so tall, settled for his elbow to draw him near. "Tell me, have you ever heard of a talking whale called 'Nox'?"

Two hours later, the scene outside The Sydney Aquarium was a very different one. Now it was Slam Guru who pumped Emma's and James's hands with enthusiasm, as if they'd been friends for years. With a final goodbye, he and his entourage left.

Emma was so happy that she launched into a victory dance. She had done what no other journalist had succeeded in doing before! She, Emmalina Estafania Corazon Oakley, had scored the interview of a lifetime! But when Emma turned around, fist still pumping, hips mid-shake, she was mortified to find the source of her happiness standing behind her, watching. A look of amusement played on his lips. Emma froze.

It is one of the Laws of the Universe that when you need a big hole to swallow you up, it is never there.

"I just came back to see if you guys would like

to come to my concert. And the after party, of course." Then he gave Emma a kiss, which left her stammering and tongue tied.

"S-s-sounds wonderful. Thanks so much," she said, with a disbelieving look at James. The tickets shook in her hand.

You didn't have to be perfect to have a perfect life.

CHAPTER 14

First and last group hug.

Emma gave Katriona the signed photograph of Slam Guru and watched her friend almost faint with delight. The picture had no dedication on it, just a messy scrawl of *SlmGu* as the letters merged together. She kept the news about the free tickets to herself. Although Slam had given her and James two each, she planned on taking Alana to the concert as a surprise for her birthday. Somehow she had a feeling James would not be choosing Katriona. She most definitely did not share the fact Slam Guru had switched hotels. Emma trusted Katriona. She just didn't trust her self-control.

Alana gave her mother a huge hug. "I'm so proud," she whispered.

"Me too," said James, overhearing. "I wasn't sure you could pull it off, Emma, but somehow you did. You never cease to amaze me."

"The dress helped!" said Ling Ling, not wanting to be left out.

Katriona held the photo of Slam Guru in front of her, "I know exactly where I'm putting you tonight!" she said, winking at the face of her idol.

Alana had a long list of things she did not want to see again: like the crack above Mr Peyton's pants whenever he bent for the newspaper thrown on next door's lawn, or Mrs. Cassidy, their prying neighbor, who had the nasty habit of picking her nose. Hand over eyes, Alana warded off another visual taboo as Katriona Karovsky gave Slam's photo a long, noisy kiss. She felt ill. Even James and Emma looked uncomfortable. Katriona then placed the photo up her Rolling Stones T-shirt (revealing far more than necessary) before zipping her jacket.

Too late. It was official. Alana was scarred for life.

"Time to celebrate!" whooped Ling Ling.

...

The nightclub pulsed with strobe lights and trance music. The boom of the bass hit Emma in the chest as soon as she entered. The Sub Club (so-called because architects used genuine submarine parts for the decor) attracted a diverse following, from film producers and body piercers to high-fashion stylists. Anybody with a creative streak in search of a good time went "Subbing." Although it was Emma's first time at the club, it was a favorite haunt of Katriona and Ling Ling, and even James, who entertained the occasional out-of-town guest. What The Sub Club did best was surprise you. You never knew what was going to happen, or who was going to be there. It kept people coming back for more.

Emma felt slightly claustrophobic as she squeezed past dancers. Their frenetic shadows played on the walls like jigsaw pieces, oddly lit and unwhole. That she was away from her computer made it even worse. But she was determined to celebrate the biggest achievement of her career. She could write up the interview with Slam Guru later. She even had a few phrases lined up in her mind, jostling for attention like nervous racehorses at the gate. But she made an effort to push them all aside. Tonight she was going to have fun. Even if it killed her.

The waitress (dressed as a naval officer, of course) showed them to their "booth," a private space modeled on a submarine cabin. It even had its own periscope. From here they could observe the club without the usual noise which made conversation impossible.

"I'd like to propose a toast," said James, lifting his glass. "To the only woman I know who has more luck than the Irish."

"To Emma!" they cheered, clinking glasses.

There is a mathematical equation in bars all over the world, that the total number of drinks you are likely to consume, equals the number of people within your party. Emma did not know or care about such a calculation. What Emma *did* know was that treating, or *shouting*, as the term is known, everybody to a drink would equal more than enough fun for her. But what Emma did not count on was the tradition of everybody having a turn: after Emma paid for the first round of drinks, James paid for the second, and so on until everybody had Shouted A Round.

One drink quickly became four.

A second tradition added to Emma's downfall. It is considered very bad manners to leave before you have had a chance to pay for your round. Even worse was to time your departure for after you've had the pleasure of several free ones. So when Emma mistakenly paid for a *second* round, the friends were thrust onto a merry-go-round of rules to which they were bound by courtesy and custom.

Four drinks quickly became eight.

It was the type of equation Ling Ling's family would have adored. But where the Shus saw beauty and symmetry, Emma saw shifty shapes with vampire teeth.

An hour later, the toasts made less sense.

"To *Scents of the Sea* bubble bath!"

"To talking whales!"

"To stalking!"

"To ducks!"

By the second hour, the toasts made no sense at all.

"To YouTube!"

"To phartsmones!"

"To twits … I mean tweets!"

"To ducks!"

And by the third hour, the small metal cubicle was overflowing with love.

"You know, I love you, very the much. You are my world best friends."

"No, no, no, I love *you*!"

"I love youse. I love youse all."

"Rubber ducky, you're the one. You make bath time so much fun …" a voice warbled. The singer rocked her glass as she cuddled it close.

Emma's final memory of the night was of her and her three best friends – Katriona, Ling Ling and James – sharing a group hug.

Which was strange, because they had never done that before.

CHAPTER 15

It's a bird! It's a plane! It's... *Katriona?*

When Emma woke the next morning, her body was five steps behind her brain. Someone had replaced her head with a slab of concrete, and her tongue with a shag rug. She felt stiff and uncomfortable. Her muscles ached as if she'd run a marathon, and then been run over by a truck. Or maybe been run over by a truck, and *then* tried running a marathon. Whatever it was, it probably had something to do with sleeping in the bath. Why was she sleeping in the bath? It must have been because of last night. What happened last night? Emma struggled to make sense of it all, but it was like solving a Rubik's Cube in boxing gloves.

Alana would know.

Emma shuffled to the kitchen and sat down, noting Alana was dressed in soccer gear and eating pasta. Pasta? Pasta was not your typical breakfast food. Ah ha! Maybe it wasn't breakfast. Maybe it was lunchtime and she had slept in.

Alana watched her mother painstakingly process one thought after another. It would have been funny if it wasn't so sad. Her mom looked like she was in agony. To put her out of her misery, Alana described the events as she knew them, from when Emma arrived home.

"Auntie Ling Ling is still asleep in the living room. You got home about 3 o'clock this morning. Your clothes were soaking so you slept in the bathroom, so as not to wet your bed. I don't know where Uncle James or Auntie Katriona are, but someone's been calling you on your cell phone. It hasn't stopped quacking all day. When did you change your ringtone?"

Emma took in the pieces of information one at a time. She inspected each one with care, as if looking for stains on dirty laundry. It didn't help that she was in the machine with them on spin cycle.

What ringtone?

Emma took the hot cup of coffee from Alana with a kiss on her head and a murmur of thanks. She wandered through the living room to her study, and the source of the mysterious quacking.

Emma slept on a massive daybed squashed into the back of her study. She used her original bedroom, the one upstairs, as more of a walk-in closet, somewhere to store her clothes, shoes, and memories – Hugo tickling Alana so much she'd peed on his pillow, Hugo's hand-drawn moustache above her lip (done while she was asleep), which she'd worn a whole day before realising, Hugo dividing the Sunday newspaper into lifestyle (Emma), entertainment (Hugo), and world news (Alana). The room was altogether too full of Hugo for her to stay there, and since she spent so much time working, it was easier to have something close by to tumble into.

When Emma opened the door, she saw the reason for the quacking (which was more like a strangled "honk"), but could make no sense of it. With another backward glance to make sure, Emma shambled back to the living room to shake Ling Ling's shoulder.

"Ling Ling. Ling Ling! There's a penguin in my study. What's a penguin doing in my study?"

Ling Ling moved reluctantly, like a sloth poked with a stick. She swiped at the imaginary branch and shuffled deeper into the covers, away from the irritation.

"Ling Ling. Wake up! Why is there a penguin in my study?"

Ling Ling's response, when it came, did little to chase the fog, making it difficult to think.

"Penguin. Duck. Same-same lah."

A text message broke through the uncomprehending silence.

It was from James.

Turn on your TV. Now!

Emma switched on the TV like a woman in a dream. The news presenter. A good friend of hers. She'd had a haircut too. She was looking good. The new color suited her. With a shake of her head,

Emma struggled to focus.

"Police are looking for the perpetrators in this video recently posted on YouTube. Although it is unclear as to the women's identities owing to the pink ski masks, what *is* clear is they broke into Sydney's Aquarium, swam with the dolphins, set off a fire extinguisher in the shark tank, and stole a little penguin called Noodle. If anybody has information about the animal's whereabouts, they've been asked to contact police immediately. Authorities warn that the animal may be suffering from trauma and in need of urgent medical attention."

A second text from James, more disturbing than the first, buzzed through.

Where's Katriona?!!!

...

On the highest ledge of Sydney's most prestigious hotel, a pair of size 9 stilettos finished shuffling. The shoes were one meter apart. To balance, the person's arms were raised above their head the same distance. The figure looked like a large X. A human X flattened against the sparkling window of the Penthouse Suite. The Penthouse occupant, swishing open the thick, luxurious curtains expected 360° views of Sydney's Opera House, harbor, and iconic bridge. Instead, this is what he saw. There was a bloodcurdling yell. It was the kind of yell that raises the hair on your arms, paralyzes your limbs, and makes your body tremble.

Emma, James, and Ling Ling had no idea where Katriona was.

But Slam Guru did.

CHAPTER 16

Investigating, staking out, and sleuthing.

The first thing Alana did (after providing an anonymous tip to the police so Noodle could go home) was search for clues. The mystery of the missing Magic 8 Ball led to two suspects, but only one of them could be observed with regularity. Laura-or-Lorna turned out to be Lara, and Alana followed her like a bad smell. She did so with a flair Katriona would have envied. If anyone had suggested the similarity, Alana would have stopped immediately, but this was stalking for a good cause. In fact, it wasn't even stalking. It was investigating, staking out, and sleuthing, she reasoned, as she hid behind a too-short potted plant. She craned her neck round the corner. She was disappointed to find Lara was not doing anything suspicious. Lara was only obsessing over a poster in her locker. And since every girl at school was obsessing over the same one, Alana had to conclude it wasn't suspicious behavior at all.

"How can you not think he's cute, Alana?" her friends moaned.

They had been moaning a lot lately. There was a lot of moaning and sighing, and even a bit of drooling since the centerfold of Jet Tierbert, the teen heartthrob guitarist, had been published in *Tracks* magazine. Cat-shaped eyes the color of dark chocolate hid behind long bangs of the same color. His high cheekbones and pointed chin added to his exotic look. There was something about his twisted smile that hinted at a secret which every girl was dying to know, but he wasn't willing to tell. All the girls in school had his poster in their locker. Everyone. Except Alana.

"He's not so *mignon*," she said with a shrug, having added another French word to her vocabulary. "I mean he's okay, but not truly *mignon*."

When *she* fell in love, it would be with someone funny and cheerful, like her dad. Not someone gloomy and mysterious in the tall-dark-handsome way Jet was. Alana felt the familiar knot in her stomach whenever she thought of her father. But his memory seemed to be fading with every passing day, like a watercolor painting – fuzzy, faraway and out of focus. She worried the watercolor painting would become increasingly indistinct, so only an abstract would remain. Her dad. A Picasso-like mish-mosh of floating eyes, sharp triangles and disembodied lips. She decided to look up "wet mop" in French tomorrow. Jet Tierbert, with his floppy bangs and dark, brooding eyes, was definitely of the "wet mop" variety. She instantly felt better.

When Alana shared her discoveries, or non-discoveries as it turned out, the girls were studying in the library with piles of books all over the table. This was the only part of school where the traffic and bustle of King Street didn't penetrate. If it had, Mrs. Heller the librarian would have admonished it with an emphatic "Shhhh!" as she did all noise-makers. Instead, all that could be heard was the rustle of paper and the muffled footsteps of borrowers on the thick carpet.

Year Seven, the girls discovered, was much more interesting than Year Six, but it was much harder too. The teachers were very fond of talking about independent learning, and being responsible, and getting organized, and did not look kindly on the research technique of *Googling*.

"But how does anybody find anything out?" Sofia protested.

Maddie's theory was that teachers wanted them to suffer the same way they had, before the internet and cars and running water made life so much easier. "My mom's always going on about how hard it was back then, and saying, *You don't know how lucky you are, girl.* I suppose teachers figure it's not work if you just ask a computer."

"Well, if I had my Magic 8 Ball, I could ask it if the answer was ten," Sofia said, moodily staring at her math book. Maybe there's an upside to Sofia losing the charm, thought Alana to herself, but refrained from saying so out of kindness. From now on, Sofia would have to make more of an effort to understand math, rather than consulting the Magic 8 Ball for every answer.

Out loud, Alana asked if anyone had observed any suspicious behavior. Nobody, it seemed, had, although some interesting facts about Coach Kusmuk did emerge:

"Did you know our math teacher, Mr. Hornby, got angry at Coach Kusmuk last week for being in the staff room? He said, 'Where's your school tie, young man? If you want a teacher you can wait outside!'" Maddie said, hands on hips, glaring at an imaginary Coach Kusmuk. There was a furious "Shhh!" from the library desk.

"Yes, yes," Sofia said more quietly. "I saw Dr. Olivier tell her off the other day too. 'What on earth are you doing out of class?'" copied Sofia, looking down the doctor's haughty nose.

But it was Khalilah's impersonation of their science teacher which had them rolling on the floor in stitches with, "I heard Mr. Murray tell Coach, 'Oi, you! (Squat) Get out of here! Don't you know (squat) students (squat) aren't allowed (squat) to use the copier?'" she said in perfect mimicry, right down to the way he picked at his too-tight trousers for relief.

"Out!" came a voice, cranky and confident it would be obeyed. "I have had enough of your riff raff! If you cannot keep quiet while others study, please leave."

The girls trailed out, heads hung low, while Mrs. Heller the librarian, watched them. "I heard *her* tell the coach off too. Said students weren't allowed to borrow more than five books," whispered Maddie.

It seemed Coach Kusmuk was having a hard time convincing people she was a teacher at the school. But was it enough to make her want to steal a frivolous charm? Alana didn't think so, but she had an idea of how she could find out for sure.

CHAPTER 17

Treading the fine line between
fun, Fun, and no fun at all.

Emma loved words. It was words which first brought Emma and Hugo together. The words were: Don't worry about it. And they were spoken by Hugo to Emma in that way he had, with an undercurrent of quiet laughter. Hugo's friend, Oscar or Peter (she couldn't recall which) was not so forgiving. When she scraped the paintwork of Hugo's car with her side mirror, and then bumped it again reversing to apologize, he said a lot of words, unkind and disbelieving at the same time. But not Hugo. Hugo smiled at her Sorry's, Terribly Sorry's, and said, "Don't worry about it," looking as if he meant it.

Emma didn't know who was more shocked when the words were repeated, meeting a second time in a local pub known as *The Sando*. Although Oscar-or-Peter's eyes said, *Not you again?!*, Hugo's were full of pleasure and surprise. "Don't worry about it," he said once more, while she hopped from foot to foot, watching the bump on his head grow after she'd crashed the door of the ladies' bathroom on his skull. (What was he doing there, lurking like that?).

Hugo swept her Sorry's aside with new words: "Let's get out of here."

Hugo understood Emma's love of words. He knew she treasured them, and coddled them, and coaxed them, as she juggled them in her head for hours. So every birthday, instead of buying her a present, he wrote words down. New words. Nonsensical words. Made-up words with silly definitions she could giggle at and marvel over. It left Emma wondering again and again how she could be so lucky, and how he could be so clever. He wrote the same number of words as her age, so a long list of them, with their quirky reflections on Life and The Universe, filled her birthday card. Year after year.

Zestpond – a body of water which invigorates.

Naperone – a chaperone with a sleeping disorder.

Noxu – a poisonous toad with tutu-shaped folds of skin.

Hexteria – a state of excitement experienced only by Goth teenagers.

Chucknology – the technology used for throwing boys called "Chuck."

Kisserain – an area or space used exclusively for kissing.

He'd reached twenty-eight words.

Accident, Emma saw Doctor Hoggarth write neatly and precisely in tiny letters on his death certificate. It was perhaps the silliest word of all. As if Hugo would die on purpose and leave them all behind.

As a freelance journalist, Emma should have been logical, organized, and well read. But as James her work partner found out, this was far from the case. While Emma was a voracious reader, what she chose to read was often off topic. And when she did write, Emma used whatever was at hand: a napkin, the back of an electricity bill, even Alana's homework until Alana herself said Enough Was Enough and cordoned the creativity to one area of the house. Emma's study, as a result, filled with paper. Her solution was to use their plastic Christmas tree, a huge spiky thing too complicated to dismantle, as a three-dimensional notice board. Amongst the baubles and tinsel, odd bits of paper and napkins hung from its branches in disjointed sentences.

"But what about Christmas?" Alana wailed.

"I'll just take the paper off. We can push the tree out when we need it. See. It will be all ready to go," Emma said chirpily. "It's not like I'll work over the holidays."

But pushing the tree ended up being too difficult to do. And pulling it, even harder. The tree was altogether too wide for the study door and too tall for the ceiling. So every December, the Oakleys made use of a small, potted pine propped up on the coffee table, and then increasingly lower heights as it grew. The plastic tree, covered in words, remained in Emma's study, where it was forever Christmas.

Emma shuffled around the tree, looking for the right phrase to describe Slam Guru. She found it, hidden under a reindeer whose nose had fallen off. *Probably Rudolph*, she thought to herself absentmindedly. Emma snatched down the words (written on the back of an unpaid parking ticket) and typed them into the computer. In the next room she could hear Katriona and Ling Ling replaying the YouTube video of their marine escapade.

"How can you tell that's not you?"

"Because my butt isn't that big."

Ling Ling wisely refrained from saying, Well actually it *is*. Instead she said, "Well it's not *my* butt."

"It's not mine, either."

"I don't know how either of you can tell," Emma said, having been drawn in by their raised voices. Katriona and Ling Ling were standing side by side, staring first at their bottoms, and then the video for confirmation. "We're in our underwear, it's dark, and we're wearing pink ski masks – which I told you to get rid of last time."

"I'm sentimental."

Emma *harrumphed* her disbelief. "What I don't understand is how you even found Slam Guru again."

"You can be very chatty after a few drinks," Katriona said with a shifty look.

"Especially when she spikes them."

"You what?!"

Katriona was very defensive. "It's safe. They use it on horses. Or they will after the clinical trials are complete."

"People. Horses. Same-same, lah," said Ling Ling.

"Katriona, how could you? Did you see what I did? What *we* did, because we were drunk? And thanks, now I know I was drugged too."

"It was a lot of Fun. You said you wanted to have Fun, not just fun," Katriona said somewhat peevishly.

Emma gave up. Throwing her hands in the

air, she left her friends to debate the definition of Fun (a nose piercing) versus fun (stargazing in the park). After the other night, (once Emma had had time to recover) Alana sat her down and gave her a Good Talking To. If an alcoholic drink claimed to be eighty proof, she said, the percentage of alcohol was forty percent. If one drink referred to one shot, half a glass of wine or one beer, then four shots would make her mom feel very tipsy. Very tipsy indeed, Emma agreed. She herself could attest to it. Drinking too much, too fast, could kill you, Alana continued seriously, which was why people vomited or passed out (or both) before this could happen. This was the body's way of protecting itself from too much alcohol. Emma didn't need telling twice. She saw how quickly the evening had slipped from fun to Fun and then to no fun at all. She vowed never to even look at another drink.

Emma mentally pushed her sleeves up as she thrust all thoughts of alcohol, vomiting, and dropping dead from her mind. She took a seat at her computer.

Instead of the interview transcript, a new screen had mysteriously appeared.

It was flashing a message.

"Katriona! Ling Ling! WHAT IS *HOOKUP?*"

CHAPTER 18

Soppy love song vs. sleuthing... It's a no-brainer!

On days when Alana did not have P.E. with Coach Kusmuk, she continued to observe her whenever possible. She did the same with Lara. But she did not see any superstitious tendencies in either one. At least, not in the beginning. Coach Kusmuk continued to march and bark orders as if she was in the army. When she wasn't yelling at people (usually Sofia), or moaning about childhood obesity, her favorite activity was seizing Inappropriate Items for her Confiscation Cupboard. Lara spent most of her time alone, as shy and unobtrusive as ever. Since the theft, she had taken to rushing to the toilets at odd intervals. Alana wondered why, if Lara was so sick, she didn't go to the school clinic, until she herself had to visit the nurse.

"Come in! Come in!" Nurse Cathy said as soon

as Alana entered the clinic, smartly closing the book, *A Step-by-Step Guide to Disease* and placing it on the shelf next to *Brain Surgery for Dummies*.

Alana was shown the kind of courtesy reserved for five-star hotel guests. Her simple cut on the knee was examined with grave concern. Nurse Cathy eyed the rest of Alana's body speculatively. There could be any number of diseases lurking in Alana's skin, bone, tissue, heart, blood, and chest. The nurse licked her lips at the prospect and stared hungrily for symptoms.

"I can have you bandaged up in a jiffy. You'll be as good as new," she promised, with a vague wave at another patient wrapped head to toe, like a mummy. This particular "mummy" sat in a large armchair, cemented in a meditative pose. Hands rested on knees, feet firmly planted on the floor, mouth set in a permanent "O." *Patient X*, the medical chart announced. A silent mountain of plaster and gauze. Alana looked at the white specter in alarm.

"Just a Band-Aid will do, thanks."

"Oh, don't mind this old thing," Nurse Cathy assured her, moving to stand on top of the *S.O.S.* carved crudely on the floor by the mummy's big toe. "I've just been practicing."

It was no wonder Lara didn't go to the clinic if she was unwell. Nobody did, if they could help it. And all the hypochondriacs discovered a miraculous cure.

The only thing Coach Kusmuk and Lara had in common was catching Alana staring at them. *(Darn, those potted plants were too short!)* Coach Kusmuk's expression was always suspicious and resentful, as if she knew Alana was aware of how much of a struggle it was for her to be taken seriously, while Lara's was fearful, and (Alana liked to imagine) tinged with guilt. Alana realized they would have to take a proactive approach. They would have to lay a trap.

But laying a trap was not going to be easy. Each subject teacher set the students project work and group assignments. This kept the girls very busy. Very soon, it seemed, it would be the school holidays. Alana was piqued she was no nearer to solving the mystery than when she had begun. Sofia had given up on finding the charm again. Her mood ring was now a deep green, which matched her calm and serene temper.

Today, the four girls were working on an original composition in one of the rehearsal rooms. Their music teacher, country-music-hopeful Jack Stratt, had asked them to write their own song. Alana nicknamed him Jack Strutt, for the distinctive way he walked, part-cowboy and part-catwalk model. He also spoke with an American accent, which Alana suspected was fake. Every five seconds he smoothed his thick, wavy blonde hair.

"Good songs tell stories," Jack drawled, swaggering around the classroom. "I'm not gonna tell you what stories you should tell, but the ones that truly move people are the ones that are most real. So write from your heart. Share your pain … your joy … your soul …" His eyes looked heavenward. "And you'll touch people," he said, turning his blue eyes to look poignantly at the students while reaching out a hand. Some of the girls sighed.

"You've got to be kidding me!" muttered Alana to herself. "He's like a walking *cliché*!"

So far, Khalilah and Maddie had written parts for the flute and violin, while Sofia scribbled notes on how she could play drums. All of them had their own version of what the lyrics should sound like, but the results so far were much too soppy for Alana's liking. This made her slightly unhappy, since she would be the one singing them while playing guitar. She felt sure it was because of Jet Tierbert's latest hit, "Don't Leave Me," from his album, "Heartbroken." Maddie played a suspiciously similar melody, which had Khalilah and Sofia clapping with enthusiasm. They don't even realize they're doing it! Alana groaned quietly, staring at her lovestruck friends.

Alana felt like the only black cloud in a room full of mushy marshmallows.

"Hey, I've been thinking how we could check if Coach Kusmuk or Lara is superstitious," Alana said to shift her mood. She felt confident no one would hear their plotting in the soundproof room.

"Oh Alana, I don't know. I don't think I can be bothered anymore, you know?" Sofia said, her eyes darkening with sadness.

But Alana persisted, and convinced Sofia and the others they should at least try. They would do three tests. The first test (a very simple one) involved setting up a ladder in the school corridor to see if Coach Kusmuk or Lara went under it, or around it.

"People who don't want bad luck won't walk under a ladder," Alana said with confidence.

The second test would use Jinx, Katriona's cat, who was black. Most superstitious people, Alana explained, would be keen to avoid him.

"Are you sure it's not because he has three legs and eczema?" Maddie asked with a wry smile.

The third test was more difficult to arrange. Somehow they had to get Lara or Coach Kusmuk to open an umbrella … indoors.

"It's supposed to be bad luck to open an

umbrella inside. Right, Sofia?" Alana said, looking to her friend, who nodded in confirmation.

"Sure, but unless it's raining *inside*, why would they even want to?" Maddie pointed out.

Khalilah's eyes lit up. "Ooo-oo-ooh!"

Alana knew that look. It was the same look her mom's friends got whenever they had an idea. Usually a stupid one in which someone got thrown in jail. But it was days later she remembered this. Days too late.

"Don't worry, Alana. With the school fundraiser coming up, I think Maddie and I can help with that one. Leave it to us," Khalilah said with a wink at Maddie's startled face. Maddie didn't know what Khalilah had in mind. She didn't like the gleam in her eyes either, but she nodded all the same. She would do anything to help their friend. "Shall we get on to the lyrics, then? What have you got, Maddie?"

Maddie cleared her throat nervously before starting a soulful melody.

"Okay. It's not very good, but anyway …

When I look into your eyes.

I get so lost inside.

You're all I've ever dreamed of, ooh.

Who knew you could be true?

I'm drowning. It's true. Drowning in you."

The three girls clapped loudly as Maddie gave a self-conscious bow and quickly sat down.

"I can go next," Sofia said, excitement dancing in her eyes. She launched into a pop version of her song.

"Ooh I'm the one, the one for you, baby. Only you don't know it yet.

I'm your sunshine. I'm your world.

Your everything. Only you don't know it yet.

Turn around and open your eyes. Ooh baby. I tell no lies.

The only one for you."

Alana and her friends couldn't help but whoop and laugh at Sofia's infectious enthusiasm.

"Okay. Now me," said Khalilah, giving a false cough which made them giggle.

"Yo, yo, now come on.

You're like a madness.

Now, now, now, come on.

It's gettin' so bad, this.

You've got me thinkin' of you, night and day.

Oh, why dontcha just take me away?

There's a fire in my veins and I'm no longer breathin'.

You got me twisted and a-he-he-he-heavin'.

Yo, yo, yo, madness.

Word."

Khalilah finished the rap with a windmill, landing on her knees with a dramatic flourish. It was no surprise she got the loudest applause of all.

"Your turn, Alana," she said, puffing.

"I can't wait to hear what you've come up with. I bet you've got something great, what with your dad, and everything," Maddie enthused. In answer to Khalilah's puzzled expression, she explained, "Mr. Oakley was a successful songwriter. Before he passed away, that is. One of his songs was even made into a jingle for that soda advertisement. You know the one with the surfers –"

"– and the platypus, yes, yes, that's one of my favorites; it's so adorable! And the tune is so catchy. Wow, Alana," Khalilah said, clapping her hands in excitement, "let's hear it!"

"Mine's a bit different to all of yours, but here goes," Alana said, suddenly worried.

"*I miss you. Your cute eyes and puffy cheeks used to make me smile.*

You loved your food. You loved to run. You loved to hide and sleep. Why couldn't you have stayed a while?

Choo choo. Soft and furry.

Choo choo. Cute and cuddly.

Choo choo. Oh how I miss you.

Choo choo," Alana trailed off.

There was a long silence.

"That was deadly, Alana," Maddie finally said.

"Yeah, it was … sweet. Really sweet," added Sofia, giving Alana's arm a pat.

"Some hardcore rock for sure," said Khalilah, nodding vigorously.

But Alana wasn't fooled. "You hated it," she said. Each girl took care to avoid her eyes.

"No!"

"Well, ..."

"Not really ..."

Maddie gave the others a warning glance. "It just ... doesn't have the same vibe as ours. You know? But that doesn't make it bad, or anything."

Alana scrunched up her piece of paper and threw it into the bin. She resigned herself to the fact that she would be singing a love song ... just not one about a deceased hamster. If she was honest, she was happy to escape. She would much rather work on solving the mystery.

"Okay, I think I'll leave the icky stuff to you guys. I'm gonna go catch me a thief," she said with an exaggerated Stratt-like drawl. She walked out of the rehearsal room with a cowboy's lope. "See ya, pardners. Wish me *bonne chance*. That's Frenchie fer good luck," and with a *pow* from her cocked fingers, she was off.

CHAPTER 19

A second chance at love.

After Emma got over the initial shock of discovering what HookUp was, she looked at the website (and the responses to her biodata) with equal measures of excitement and horror.

"The great thing about it, though, is that it looks like you, but at the same time it doesn't. It looks even better," enthused Katriona, proud of her computer skills.

"Well, I do *look* younger," Emma said dubiously.

"That's what I said. Better. Way better."

"But my body doesn't look like *that*."

"Doesn't matter."

"In fact, it's NEVER looked like that."

"Your body. This body. Same-same lah!" Ling Ling chipped in.

"Who cares?" agreed Katriona. "Look how many hits you've got. This one sounds good! Listen to this one …" and proceeded to read one response after another.

"But don't you see? They're all responding to this woman, *LegsEleven,* who isn't even real! What do I know about bungee jumping, rock climbing, or hang gliding? I've never done any of those things. And calling my car a monster truck is a plain lie."

"*LegsEleven* IS real. Okay, so the details aren't completely true, but the gist of them is. You *are* fun loving, you *are* soft hearted, and that car of yours *is* a beast," Katriona said, winking at Emma's weak grin.

"Oh, it's just too pathetic. I can't do this. What happened to the old-fashioned way?" Emma said, burying her burning face in her hands.

Ling Ling looked stern. "What, like meeting someone? You have to have a social life for that. Let's face it, Emma. Who do you *see* apart from us, James, and Alana?"

Emma looked at Katriona and Ling Ling a little uncertainly, as she tried to count the number of people.

"Well, there's the postman, but he doesn't stay very long, and I tend to miss him by the time I check for mail; then there's the lovely waiter at the café where I grab a cup of coffee, although he's gone back-packing to Peru. I used to go to Book Club, but I haven't been for a while, and … and …" And then she realized there *was* no one. No one at all. For three years it had been just her and her computer, interviewees like Slam Guru (although rarely as gorgeous or available), her lovely friends, and her Alana, Alana who kept life smooth and ripple-free. When Emma looked at life like that – with a magnifying glass rather than binoculars that kept things far away, and blurry, *and safe* – she felt a bit sad. And rather lonely. And pushing away the thoughts did not make them go.

"This is how it's done now. Come on. Just try it. For a bit of a laugh. What could possibly go wrong?"

And so, because Emma had a short memory for all the things that *had* gone wrong, she gave in. After all, she was just going to do a bit of writing.

Different writing to what she normally did, true, but it was still writing.

Dating, she knew nothing about, but writing? She knew how to do *that*.

And *PeterPan* sounded ... interesting ...

CHAPTER 20

Yes, Coach. No, Coach.
Three bags full.

The school held several fundraisers throughout the year. Everybody pitched in to create a fun event. There was always Hook-the-Duck, Beat-the-Goalie, and the traditional Chock-Chock-Chockie-Wheel of Fortune with prizes donated from local stores. The most successful stall last year was the Water Dunker. Students lined up for a chance to hit a target, which, if hit hard enough, made one of their teachers fall into a pool of water. In the lead-up to the fundraiser, the school was a confusion of scaffolding and decorations as people prepared their stalls. It was the perfect time for Alana and her friends to stage their daring plan.

Everything was in place. A ladder stood in a narrow hallway where both Coach Kusmuk and Lara would have to pass. A few meters beyond the ladder, Alana waited with Jinx, Katriona's soot-colored cat. As for the final superstition, Khalilah and Maddie assured Alana they had everything under control. All Sofia had to do was offer the suspects an umbrella. They would take care of the rest.

When the bell for class rang, the tight passageway became a bottleneck, as people were forced over and under the ladder. Coach Kusmuk, Alana saw, had no trouble striding under the metal equipment, but Lara looked like a hounded rabbit. Too big to squeeze past it and, by the look of it, too scared to pass under it, she eventually grabbed the ladder, and with a herculean effort, heaved it out of the way.

In the meantime, Alana put Jinx down in place and disappeared. Lara's face, when she spotted the black cat, was a picture. Too many people blocked her way to go back past the ladder. Lara stood frozen and cornered. The cat looked at her with disdain. Coach Kusmuk however, had no such qualms. She had just finished confiscating yet another Inappropriate Item from a student when she spied Jinx, legs askew, licking ineffectually at his eczema.

"I swear this place is more like a zoo than a school," the coach said, scooping Jinx up in one movement and muttering about the local animal shelter under her breath.

From her vantage point, hidden by the swell of students, Alana took note of their different reactions.

Jinx, however, had no intention of going back to the Cat Protection Society, where it was rumored vital bits got cut off. With a quick flick of his tail, he bounded out of Coach Kusmuk's arms before she could stop him. Alana watched him run away with a sigh. She wasn't too worried. She knew he would race all the way home like a homing pigeon, after "visiting" a few ladies along the way. Alana often thought Jinx should have been named Casanova. Certainly, missing a leg and having a chronic skin condition didn't stop him from siring the neighborhood's cats. She followed the pair from a safe distance, careful not to be seen.

Sofia stood waiting for Coach Kusmuk and Lara by the door of one of the school's indoor gardens. Once the first wave of people passed, she quickly put a detour sign in place. The sign, she realized too late, did not look very professional. In the rush to get it done, the girls had forgotten the "u" so it read "Detor" in rather scraggly writing. Lara was the first to arrive.

"Hi, La-ra," Sofia called in a loud, slow voice, so Khalilah and Maddie could hear her from their hiding spot. "Would You Like An Um-bre-lla?"

She offered her an umbrella as she pointed upwards. A second, makeshift sign hung askew above the doorway: "Caution. Wet Area." Lara took one nervous look at the umbrella, and rushed through the door. Coach Kusmuk was not far behind, her face stormy as usual.

Sofia again offered protection in a booming voice.

"Do I look like Mary Poppins to you?" the coach barked. Sofia quickly withdrew. Minutes later the door swung open again.

Coach Kusmuk and Lara emerged dripping wet.

Sofia stood helplessly by the door. She offered the umbrella a second time, but neither of them took it. Alana arrived. Her mouth dropped open. *This was their plan?*

A shrill ring cut through the heavy silence.

"Did it work? Hello? Alana? Can you hear me? Did it work?" Khalilah's voice could be heard rising tinnily from the phone.

Coach Kusmuk, thin rivulets of water tracking lines down her face, snatched the mobile from Alana's unresisting fingers. She pocketed it. Her mouth a thin line.

"Well now, what's going on here?" a voice boomed. It was Mr. Murray, the girls' science teacher.

Khalilah and Maddie came rushing in, empty buckets banging against their knees as they ran.

"Oh, Mr. Murray!" Khalilah exclaimed, quickly taking in the scene and its terrifying ramifications. "It's all a big mistake. We were doing a science experiment after being totally inspired by your explanation about space and anti-matter, and tried to apply the same principles to water and, and …"

"And we tried to make anti-water," said Sofia, proudly.

"Anti-water?" Mr. Murray's bushy eyebrows disappeared.

"Yes. As in un-wet. We were testing to see if we could make un-wet water," Maddie said. Even in saying it, you could tell she was having a hard time believing it herself.

Mr. Murray unconsciously squatted to release the tension from his tight trousers, which only made them tighter. "Well, goodness. (Squat). Un-wet water, eh? There's a first. (Squat). I admire your initiative, but it seems clear to me your principle is rather unsound. (Squat). But by golly, I do admire your creativity. (Squat). This is what the school strives for, after all. Inquiring minds, and all that. (Squat). A pity about the mess, but luckily the plants seems to have taken the brunt of it …"

"But, but, what about us?" Coach Kusmuk spluttered. "They deserve at least a detention!"

Mr. Murray held up a warning hand. "No, no, (squat) I wouldn't dream of squashing the thrill of discovery. But," he said, looking sternly at the four friends, "this boy is right. (Squat). You owe them an apology," and with one final, deep squat that made him look like a frog poised to spring, he waddled away, chuckling to himself about anti-matter and un-wet water.

He still thought Coach Kusmuk was a student! And a boy! And Coach Kusmuk knew they knew.

The P.E. teacher's expression was thunderous. She turned to Alana and held up her phone. Coach Kusmuk's hand, like the rest of her, shook with rage.

"If you want this back, you will see me in my office with one of your parents. Until then, it will stay locked in the Confiscation Cupboard," she barked before striding through the door.

"We're sorry, Lara. We didn't mean you to get wet," Alana said to the girl who was standing in a miserable puddle. "Why didn't you use the umbrella?"

"It's bad luck to open an umbrella indoors. I thought everyone knew that," Lara said with a sullen look, and slipped away.

The four girls looked at each other. They now knew who was the more superstitious of the two, but it still didn't prove she had taken the Magic 8 Ball charm.

"Un-wet water? Seriously?" Khlalilah suddenly asked, eyes glinting with laughter.

Sofia, hands on hips, replied, "Dunking Coach Kusmuk? Do you two have a death wish?"

Maddie shook her head and pointed at Khalilah. "You should have heard the original idea. You're lucky this was only water!"

Alana put her arms around them all and led them out the door. "It's not my ideal way of sneaking a peek at the Confiscation Cupboard, but it'll do. And next time, Khalilah, if you have another Bright Idea, remind me not to listen."

CHAPTER 21

Emma chooses an adventure
over tea.

Emma avoided her study for a whole day. As soon as she woke up, she went straight outside and puttered around the garden (if "puttering" was watering plants refusing to die – weeds – and trimming the rhododendron bushes). After gardening, she went inside and tidied the living room. She even cleaned the kitchen and baked a tray of muffins, which she (unusually) sat to watch rise. This probably explained why they emerged a golden brown color, like the recipe promised. When she *did* summon the courage to walk into her study, she spent ten minutes rearranging the papers on her desk into senseless piles. Then the bowls and plates of half-eaten food were collected and put in the kitchen sink. Returning, she looked at the scraps of paper on the Christmas tree without seeing them, her eyes drawn like a magnet to the silent machine on her desk.

Last night she sent a response to *PeterPan*. Emma was dying to find out what, if anything, *PeterPan* had said. But also slightly afraid. She now deeply regretted the message she'd typed. Didn't her mother always warn her that you only got one chance to make a first impression, and yet she'd probably blown it with, "What's a nice guy like you doing in a place like this?" So L-A-M-E! Emma cringed just thinking about it.

Emma's fingernails tapped the table. It was already late afternoon. She couldn't remember the last time she had taken a day off. Even on days she hadn't worked, she'd always hopped onto the computer to at least check emails. Chiding herself for being so silly, she took a deep breath and looked at the screen. There was a message from *HookUp*. It was *PeterPan*!

PeterPan: It's the only place I know people like me for me. Not because of what I look like, who I am, or what I do.

Emma smiled as she sat down. He sounded nice. Sensitive, even. She had no idea if he was online, but decided to answer before she changed her mind.

LegsEleven: So why PeterPan?

Almost immediately, an answer flashed onto the screen. He was there!

PeterPan: Young at heart? Why LegsEleven?
Do you play Bingo often?

Emma smiled as she typed.

LegsEleven: Yes, every night after my bowl of prunes, they wheel me out for some entertainment.

Then, because she was anxious to let him know she wasn't really a pensioner with false teeth and possible bowel issues in an Old Folk's Home, she quickly added: *(Kidding).*

PeterPan: Careful. I hear Bingo can get pretty rough. LOL.

LOL? Emma thought to herself. Never had she felt so out-of-touch with the world and modern technology. She glanced at the Christmas tree for inspiration. The song "Frosty the Snowman" came unbidden to mind. A feisty-looking snowman with a top hat, rakish grin, and walking stick which he didn't use for walking …

LegsEleven: Don't worry. I can hold my own. If anyone gives me trouble they'll meet my walking stick.

PeterPan: Ouch. Looks like I'm going to have to watch out! I was hoping the reason for your avatar was because your legs matched the rest of your body …

Which looks great, by the way ☺*…*

Emma looked at the smiley emoticon and wished she knew the button on her computer which did that. She made a mental note to ask Katriona and Ling Ling for a crash course on Modern Communication as soon as they came over.

LegsEleven: It's called Irony. Time for me to go to bed now … 4pm already …

PeterPan: LMFO. K, nite nite grandma. Look forward to chatting again soon.

LMFO? What was that? Modern Communication, it seemed, was full of acronyms and abbreviations and strange symbols. It was like a foreign language. In a panic, she typed:

LegsEleven: Zzzzzzzzzzz …

Emma signed off with mixed emotions. There was a slight buzzing in her brain which she hadn't felt for a long time. She felt strangely high. Katriona and Ling Ling were right. It *was* fun.

If she wasn't careful, it might even turn out to be Fun.

Alana arrived home with a bang of the door. Her running footsteps pounded up the stairs, then down again. Minutes later, she wandered into the study, staring at the perfect muffin in her hand with a look of confusion.

"Are you feeling alright, Mom?"

Emma smiled.

"I feel great," she said, and was surprised to find this was true.

CHAPTER 22

Alana vs. Coach Kusmuk. Round Two.

Coach Kusmuk shoved open a door and led Alana and Emma in. The room was small and neat, just like her. A wall of shelves displayed an impressive number of trophies. One of them, according to the engraving, was first place for "Gumnastics." Somehow, Alana couldn't imagine Coach Kusmuk laughing at the mistake. A pair of plastic office chairs stood at attention in front of her desk. Coach Kusmuk struggled with the bundle of files in her arms. Emma rushed to help.

"Here, let me do that, you poor thing. They shouldn't make someone like you carry so much, but then," she said, lowering her voice to a conspiratorial whisper, "I've heard the coach is a total idiot, so I'm not surprised."

Coach Kusmuk stiffened. The files landed on the desk with a loud *bang*. Not surprisingly, her smile did not reach her eyes as she thrust out a hand to introduce herself, "Coach Kusmuk. Or total idiot. Whichever you prefer."

Adults have a knack for saying "Uh huh," and "Yes" and "Really?" with just the right tone and inflection, so you would never know they weren't listening. So when Alana briefed her mom for the meeting, all Emma heard was: "Coach Kusmuk, *blah, blah, blah,* prat, *blah, blah, blah,* took my phone, *blah, blah, blah.*" And Emma said, "Uh huh," and "Yes" and "Really?" with just the right tone and inflection.

Adults really should pay more attention.

But then Emma said the one thing which seemed to erase all ills:

"Is that a photo of Cristina Ibrahmovic? Goodness, she seems so young there."

Coach Kusmuk was surprised. "You know her?"

"Well, I wouldn't say *know.* We got trapped in the same elevator once. Stuck there for five hours …"

The thing about Emma was she was sweet, and

funny, and good at telling stories. *Very good* at telling stories. And she always knew the right one to tell. It made people lower their guard and open their heart. Within five minutes, Coach Kusmuk and Emma were sharing memories of the talented gymnast-turned-icon, and how Ibrahmovic had transformed both their lives.

"Of course, Cristy's commitment to bringing gymnastics training to underprivileged kids was always going to be a challenge, but you know her, she's a real fighter, and when *Champion* magazine agreed to let me write a piece about what she was doing, well, it just snowballed – exposure, sponsorship, you name it, everything clicked into place."

"So *you* were the one who wrote that article in *Champion*? That changed her life. It changed *my* life. I got a scholarship when her foundation received more funding." Coach Kusmuk's voice held a new note of admiration.

Emma waved it off with a flick of her hand. "It was just the right article, in the right magazine, at the right time. If only I could be so lucky every time, right, Alana?" deftly bringing the conversation back to the reason for their meeting.

Coach Kusmuk beamed at Alana. The transformation was so dramatic that Alana checked she wasn't looking at someone else. "Hmmm, yes. Alana. She did very well during her assessment, you'll be pleased to know. I've recommended her for our Elite Sports Squad, which starts next year. As for her phone, I think Alana's learned her lesson about using it during school hours. It's certainly not something we encourage, you understand."

Emma nodded, and nudged Alana so she could show signs of repentance. Alana assumed a contrite expression.

"Let me get my key for the Confiscation Cupboard. It's a treasure trove of booty, let me tell you," Coach Kusmuk said with pride. "I inherited it from the previous coach, who inherited it from the one before that, and so on. We've probably got about five generations' worth of stuff in here," she said as she slid back a shelf of trophies to reveal a rickety steel locker standing as high as the ceiling. It was packed with all sorts of things: paintball guns, slingshots, fart bombs, playing cards, silly putty, martial arts weapons, and Indian peace pipes – it was all there. Every object ever taken from the troubled teens of the Police Boys' Club, and more recently, the students of Gibson High was in that cupboard. Alana looked at the impossible tower of impounded items. How would she know if Sofia's charm bracelet was there? There were hundreds of things. Neatly stacked like packed fruit or a pyramid of tin cans. So perfectly placed that one false move would bring the whole thing down.

With a sharp intake of breath, Emma moved in for a closer look. "Oh, my! That looks just like my old *Whammo Yoyo*. I'm almost sure it's the same one I, uh, lost ages ago, and oh, I can't believe it could still be around. May I?"

Before Coach Kusmuk could answer, Emma was already reaching for the vintage toy and pulling it toward her.

There is a moment in time when Time itself seems to stand still. As if the world is taking a deep breath before letting out a loud, shocked gasp. As soon as Emma had her *Whammo Yoyo* in hand, there was one such pause. After that, there was a ripple effect as first the *Rockem Sockem Robot*, next to the *Super Stretch Slinky*, tipped. Row upon row of dangerous detritus fell over. Over and off. The *ratatatat* of falling debris got faster and louder as more things dropped. The paintball guns, slingshots, fart bombs, playing cards, silly putty, martial arts weapons, and marbles made a terrific racket. A toy monkey in red-and-white-striped trousers and a yellow vest began playing the cymbals, its fallen body convulsing on the floor.

The sound left a ringing in their ears.

Coach Kusmuk did not smile at Emma's Sorry's, Terribly Sorry's, as the three of them scrambled on the floor to gather everything up. Although she did say, "Don't worry about it." But not the way Hugo said it. It was more like, Don't. Worry. About. It. Clipped and short. And her eyes said Don't. Touch. A. Thing. as she silently handed Alana her phone.

With her long-lost yoyo in one hand, and Alana's hand in the other, Emma fled the room.

CHAPTER 23

Alana finds the culprit!

The mystery of the missing Magic 8 Ball charm had reached a turning point. The girls took turns to check the scanned photo of Coach Kusmuk's Confiscation Cupboard, which Alana managed to snap before running with her mom from the room.

"She doesn't look very happy, does she?" Maddie observed, looking at their P.E. teacher glaring at the camera, surrounded by hundreds of Inappropriate Items. Maddie promptly zoomed out and searched a different part of the image for a hint of the charm. None of them could see it anywhere.

Coach Kusmuk was looking less likely to be the culprit. All the evidence so far, pointed at Lara, whose trips to the bathroom took on a suspicious air.

"I've noticed Lara seems to rush to the bathroom

whenever she has to make a decision."

"Funny, now you mention it, I think you're right. She always goes to the bathroom before choosing her library books."

"And she doesn't take forever to order lunch anymore. She seems to know exactly what she wants –"

"– *after* going to the bathroom," Sofia said as realization dawned.

"She passed our superstition test on all three counts, too. I also overheard her get angry at someone for writing her name in red ink. Said it was bad luck, and made the person trace over it in black," Maddie said.

"Although it could be a coincidence."

But, as mystery stories had shown Alana, it didn't pay to ignore even the slightest coincidence. "She's definitely our Number One Suspect. I think I'm going to do a little bit of investigating in the girls bathroom when I get the chance," she said, a thoughtful look on her face.

The opportunity came sooner than expected.

Their next class was math, and Mr. Hornby asked them to work in pairs for their study on probability. Alana surprised Lara by suggesting they be partners. Lara, after a slight hesitation, agreed.

Just like Mr. Murray, who frequently liked to digress and talk about unrelated topics (hence his previous discussion on anti-matter), Mr. Hornby also meandered from topic to topic. But while Mr. Murray's detours took him to the edges of the universe and beyond, Mr. Hornby's tangents seemed to contain a world's worth of trivia.

"Did you know that the chance of you dying on your way to collect your lottery ticket is greater than your chance of winning?" he said with an eager smile. The Year Seven students were not sure whether it was the thought of their impending doom or the numerical implications which caused him the most excitement. "Probability is everywhere. It surrounds us wherever we go, and whatever choices we make."

A few of the students glanced around

nervously, as if trying to catch a glimpse of this mathematical shadow.

"Now in pairs, I would like you to flip a coin and record your results. You're to flip it a total of fifty times, and count how many times you get heads, and how many times you get tails. Then we'll come together to discuss it. "

A couple of desks away, Sofia moaned about her missing Magic 8 Ball. She always felt the loss more keenly in math than any other time.

Mr. Hornby drifted over and drew up a chair. "What seems to be the problem?"

Perhaps it was the fatherly way in which he sat patiently, hands in lap, or it could have been the kindness of his expression, filling his warm brown eyes, but whatever it was, Sofia began telling him the reason for her unhappiness. When Sofia was agitated, she spoke quickly without pause, and virtually no punctuation, so her words linked together like a long chain. Barely taking a breath, Sofia spoke about her various charms (which Mr. Hornby dutifully admired), the reasons she wore them, and the specialness of her Magic 8 Ball, which said *yes*, *no*, and *maybe*, in a multitude of ways that helped her decide.

"Well now, this is simply wonderful!" Mr. Hornby declared. At Sofia's hurt expression, he rushed on to say, "No, no, not that you have lost such a precious object, but that you can see the magic in numbers which are represented in this lucky Magic 8 Ball you've just described. This is exactly the kind of passion that warms my heart, my dear. And now," his voice dropped to a whisper, "I'm going to share with you some of probability's special secrets."

Sofia did not know what to say. She would never have described herself as passionate about numbers. Frightened, perhaps. Horrified, sometimes. But passionate? No. Never. However, Mr. Hornby, with his soothing voice, pulled away the mysterious fog that made numbers appear puzzling and secretive. He teased away her fear. It was like a parting of cobwebs. For the first time ever, Sofia *understood*. As the clatter of coins continued in the background, Sofia looked at the squiggles and marks on her paper, and they made sense for the first time. The math teacher's eyes twinkled as he looked at Sofia's glowing face. Both were thinking the same thing.

Magic!

Alana, meanwhile, sneaked out of the classroom to follow Lara, who had slipped to the bathroom yet again. She eased the door open carefully, so as not to make a noise, and placed her feet on the tiles, toes first. All but one of the cubicles was free. Through the closed door, Alana could hear somebody mumbling and moaning. Alana inched forward. She became aware of how her chest rose and fell as she attempted to muffle the sound of her breathing. Taking the stall to the occupied cubicle's left, she pressed an ear to the wall.

"Should I give it back?" a faint voice could be heard saying. There was a groan of frustration, and then the question repeated. "Should I give it back?"

Alana decided to stand on the toilet seat to take a peek at next door's occupant. With the wall for support, she was able to climb up and balance without difficulty, but to observe Lara, the awkward angle stretched Alana's body into a precarious diagonal line, one meter off the ground. Alana clutched the top of the cubicle wall with sweaty fingers as her toes balanced on their tips.

As Alana peered over the top she could see Lara sitting on the closed seat of the toilet. Sofia's missing charm bracelet was in her hand. Every now and then, Lara shook the Magic 8 Ball charm in increasing frustration. *The Magic 8 Ball was not giving her the answer she wanted.*

"Oh, you stupid thing! I wish I'd never taken you!" Lara's tear-streaked face suddenly turned toward the ceiling. It changed to one of shock, and then horror, when she saw Alana's face.

Both girls erupted from their respective cubicles. Lara defensive, as Alana went on the attack. But it didn't take long for Lara to crumple in defeat, and begin sobbing, tears and mucus streaming down her face. Alana looked at her with a mixture of pity and anger. It was obvious Lara was sorry for what she had done, but Alana was still upset on her friend's behalf.

"Why did you take it? You knew it was special to Sofia."

"I need it more than she does. You don't know what it's like being me. I never know what to choose, what I should do, which way to go. I always feel stuck. And then Sofia seemed to have the answer. This Magic 8 Ball tells Sofia the answer to *everything*," Lara gestured wildly. "You heard her. The Magic 8 Ball never lies."

Alana's heart softened. She *did* know what it was like not being able to choose, and being afraid of making the wrong decision, but her fear never left her paralyzed. She just made her choice and hoped for the best, convinced no matter what happened, good or bad, right or wrong, she could live with the consequences. Life was about making choices. Making mistakes was how you learned.

In a gentler voice, Alana asked, "What happens if you don't like the answer the Magic 8 Ball gives you?"

Lara sniffed noisily, "I just shake it again."

"So you keep shaking it until you get the answer you want, *the answer that's in you all along.* It's there, you know. You just have to be confident and listen to it."

For the first time since she had known her, Alana saw Lara smile. It wasn't the kind of smile you could use for a toothpaste commercial. It was more wobbly and watery, like a lukewarm rainbow struggling through a grey cloud.

But it was there.

It was a start.

...

When Lara had to return the charm bracelet to Sofia, she was so frightened of the other girl that her heart beat in her chest like a trapped bird. With a look of encouragement from Alana, her trembling hand held out the missing piece of jewelry.

"I'm so sorry," Lara whispered. "I just felt so desperate and thought your Magic 8 Ball was the answer to my problems, but I know better now. I guess I need to learn to make my own decisions from now on."

Sofia's first reaction was relief and she gave Lara's hand a squeeze. "It's okay. It was good for me to make choices of my own, even if some of them were pretty bad." A flash smiled across her pretty features. "Thanks for returning it. That was really brave." The two girls exchanged a grin. "Now," said Sofia, giving the charm a shake, "should we go to the school bakery for some muffins?" Before looking at the answer the charm had for them, Sofia shot Lara a cheeky look. "What do *you* think?"

Lara broke into a fresh sweat as she struggled for an answer. "I think, *I* think, it would be a terrible idea. I heard Miller's on duty, and last time his muffins tasted awful."

Sofia displayed the charm's answer and let out a hoot. "Good call, Lara. Good call."

No way! was its unequivocal answer.

CHAPTER 24

Food brings humanity together.

With the mystery of the Magic 8 Ball solved, Alana began her mid-year school holidays with a light heart. None of the girls was going away, and they made promises to see each other over the break. Everybody was in a jubilant mood. Not only had they survived the first six months of Year Seven but Sofia had her Magic 8 Ball back and a newfound confidence in math. The charm, she promised, would remain simply that, a charm, and not the lifeline it used to be. She said this while the trunk of the Hindu god of Luck, Ganesha, peeped from behind an amulet promising protection from the Evil Eye. After all, Sofia maintained, it didn't hurt to tip the scales of probability in your favor.

Khalilah's parents were the first to extend an invitation to their home. They had heard so much about Alana, Maddie, and Sofia and were curious to put faces to names. Khalilah had also promised Alana her dad's cooking when they'd first met on the train. A promise Alana was keen to claim.

When they visited Khalilah's home, evidence of her mom's research was everywhere. Books, files, and photocopied notes overflowed beyond the study. The bespectacled woman welcomed them warmly before disappearing into the room, with a promise to join them later for lunch. Khalilah's dad, Mr. Madzaini, shifted the remaining material into piles to make room on the table.

"Would you like to offer your guests a drink, Khalilah?"

Khalilah opened the fridge and beckoned to her friends. "So, what do you want? Soda, cranberry juice, or some very sketchy milk?" she asked, sniffing the milk container and screwing her nose in disgust.

"Khalilah!" her dad's voice was shocked. "That is not how you ask."

"Relax, *Bapa*. They're my closest friends. They

don't do fancy-schmancy."

Alana, Sofia and Maddie nodded. "No need for fancy-schmancy with us!" Sofia said.

Alana moved forward to admire some photographs hanging on the wall. Her exclamation of delight drew Mr. Madzaini's ire away from Khalilah, and with a grateful glance, the girl rushed upstairs to her room, Sofia and Maddie in tow. Alana didn't mind. As an amateur photographer, she often got tips from Uncle James, but Mr. Madzaini's work with a macro lens was a work of art. One photo showed a bug's eyes the size of her head while it feasted on nectar. Another zoomed in on a delicate drop of water poised to drop from a luscious leaf. The detail was exquisite. They launched into a complicated discussion about aperture and focal points. Mr. Madzaini had never before seen such knowledge in someone so young.

By lunch, the conversation had shifted to include everybody, covering everything from family to favorite subjects at school. Lunch was a delicious beef *rending* curry, just as Khalilah had promised. Looking back now, it seemed a lifetime ago. Khalilah's mom joined them, and she ate in short, sharp bursts. She was a woman who did not sit still for long and spent most of the meal jumping up and down to fetch things from the kitchen, or to clear the table. Like Khalilah, she wore her hair long, but her face was not as round. Kind, brown eyes took in the animated girls at the table, who hadn't stopped talking since she'd arrived. The glance she shot her husband was full of gratitude and joy.

"I can't wait for you to try some of *our* food," Maddie said, fanning her tongue from the intense spices and laughing.

"Oh, what kind of food do you usually eat, Maddie?" Khalilah's mom asked politely.

A mischievous grin tugged at the corners of the girl's mouth. "You know. The usual stuff: dingo, kangaroo, that sort of thing."

Khalilah's dad opened his mouth to protest, but was stopped by his wife placing a hand over his.

"Ah ha ha, good joke," he said weakly.

...

Maddie's family gathering ended up being much larger than even Maddie expected. But none of the girls were bothered. Alana – a frequent visitor to Maddie's home – was used to the various "aunties," "uncles," and neighbors dropping in. With five older brothers and all *their* friends, Sofia also took it in her stride. Khalilah looked around in approval. In a strange way, it felt like home to her. Both Khalilah's parents came from large families, and it was common for extended families to live at home. In Brunei, she shared a house with four of her mother's siblings and their families, as well as her grandparents. Back home, she was forever tripping over a cousin, or waiting in line for a bathroom. Khalilah missed the bustle and noise. Especially since her older brother, Jefri, was still in Brunei for religious studies. The memories brought an unexpected tear to her eye.

Maddie was at her side in an instant. "Are you okay? It's too much, isn't it," she stated rather than asked. "My family. I mean, it gets crazy here sometimes."

"No. No. No," Khalilah was quick to assure her. "It just reminds me of *my* family. Big. Noisy. Nuts," she said with a watery smile at "Uncle" Joe, who was tapping his head and yelling, "Wha's that? I can't hear ya," at "Auntie" Mo, who was nagging him to move out of the way.

Maddie didn't believe her. "You're just being polite."

"No I'm not. See that person there?" she said, pointing at a skinny girl standing in the corner with an older teen. "If I squint, she looks just like my niece, Fatin. And him, the one with the baseball cap? He plays guitar, just like my cousin, Azlan." A loud fart erupted from "Uncle" Joe, prompting a swift mock beating from "Auntie" Mo and good-natured laughter from everyone else. "See," Khalilah said, pinching her nose, "just like my Uncle Hakim."

...

At the doorstep of Sofia's home, a pungent smell just as powerful (but not as deadly) greeted Alana, Khalilah, and Maddie, which had them all guessing as to what could be on the menu. This time Sofia's family of six was playing host. Sofia's dad was a chef, but he was no ordinary cook. Mr. Luciano was part of the "experimental cuisine movement" and his cooking style was as much a scientific exploration as it was a search for extraordinary taste experiences. He designed his meals to excite each of the senses – sight, sound, smell, taste and touch – sometimes depriving the diners of one to highlight another. When the children had been much younger, Mr. Luciano had tried blindfolding them at the dinner table so as to heighten the explosions of flavor which burst in their mouths. That was until the boys took advantage of the situation and intensified the "touch experience" by exchanging secretive beatings over the head. Mr. Luciano's kitchen looked like a science lab, and he sported protective eyewear as often as an apron. Sofia's mom, a chemical engineer, was used to waiting patiently for the results of his latest research: smoking blobs of intense colors that looked more like bacterial samples than food.

Sofia's brothers had no such patience.

"Is that it?" they would cry, after gulping the carefully prepared morsels whole. Mr. Luciano would raise eyes heavenward to pray for strength, before serving up a second course of ravioli or chicken parmigiana to fill them up. Today was no different.

"Guests first!" Mrs. Luciano cried, rapping Dmitri over the knuckles. The girls smiled and quickly took a bread roll each, before passing the basket on.

"Daaaad. I didn't get any meat," one of the twins, Pepe, whined. The meat – bought especially in honor of Khalilah's visit – had been bought from a *halal* butcher, roasted on low heat for 24 hours, fashioned into sheep shapes, piped with white potato and parsnip for maximum effect, and placed on a bed of green pea *tubettini* made to look like grass.

Mr. Luciano scratched his balding head with the acetylene torch as he gave Pepe the missing portion. "I was sure I gave you two already."

"You did! You did give him two already! He hid them under his bread," the boy's twin, Bob, accused. Sure enough, *four* "sheep" stood demurely on Pepe's plate. Before anyone could reclaim them, Pepe shoved all of them in his mouth. His cheeks bulged like a hamster's.

"Pig!" Bob yelled.

Everyone but Khalilah gasped. An awkward silence settled into the room, broken only by indistinct *baaa-ing* in the background.

"Roberto Salvatore Luciano!" Mrs. Luciano's eyes flashed. Bob looked suitably chastised. The children knew they were in Big Trouble if either parent used their full name.

"Good one, Doofus," Dmitri said, clipping his little brother around the ear.

With a bang on the table and a gritted smile, Mrs. Luciano called for order. "Boys," she said, "*please!* We have guests," with a pointed look at Khalilah. But Khalilah was only chuckling merrily. "Doofus," she said to herself, savoring the way it hit the roof of her mouth, "that's a good one. *He he he.* I can't wait to use it on my brother, Jefri."

CHAPTER 25

Alana makes a shocking discovery.

When Maddie and Khalilah convinced the other two to enter their song in a local radio station's competition, the school holidays took on an air of excitement and anticipation. First prize was two free tickets and backstage passes to see Slam Guru in concert and meet him in person. This in itself was exciting, but what thrilled Alana's friends even more was that Jet Tierbert was confirmed as the supporting artist! Although it meant only two of them could go, two was better than none. They would draw straws to decide. Even Alana, who wasn't a Jet Tierbert fan, couldn't resist their enthusiasm, and she too hoped to win. They followed the radio station's blog. Their hearts rose and dipped with every rise and fall in votes. It was an emotional rollercoaster from which none of them could escape. Time would tell whether or not their song "Stormy Heart" would win first prize.

But despite the buzz and exhilaration the school break brought, Alana noticed something amiss at home. Her mom, Emma, was taking more care with her appearance. She was combing her hair, stepping into sprays of perfume and brushing her teeth regularly … *just to sit at the computer to work.* This was suspicious behavior coming from a woman who was known to spend days in the same nightie. One day, Alana noticed an American cook book, *Mom's Best,* from the library, on the kitchen bench. The page for Banana Cream Pie was earmarked. That was weird too. After her stint with the orangutans in the jungles of Borneo, and her diet of bananas, Emma had sworn off the fruit for life. Why would she be interested in *that* recipe? And almost like clockwork, Emma began a tuneless but happy hum at 8:30 every morning before rushing into the study. Perhaps the most damning evidence was the piece of paper of dictionary-type definitions Alana saw on the living room table – but not for words her mom would ordinarily need:

DLTM = don't lie to me.

(@@) = you're kidding.

:|) = it's great.

:`(= I'm going to cry.

?4U = a question for you.

(::) (::) = bandaid

911 = emergency

411 = for your information

BTDT = been there done that

SWDYT = so what do you think?

LOL = Laugh out loud

LMFO = Laugh my face off

:0 = scream(ing)

W-E = whatever

:# = kiss

:P = in your face

MFEO = meant for each other

WC = way cool

WITW = what in the world?

BW = Blair Witch = not fair

MY = miss you

OMG = Oh my goodness

OMG indeed. And it was in Ling Ling's writing. Alana's radar for Trouble perked up.

"Alright," she said, cornering Emma one day. "What's going on?"

Emma looked hounded as she fumbled for a reply. "What do you mean?"

"I mean, the makeup, the perfume, the cookbooks … wait a minute." A thought seemed to occur to her. "Do you have someone in there?"

Alana rushed into the study, searching in and around the Christmas tree. She checked behind Emma's pile of books and under the pillows of her bed. Nothing. If somebody *was* there, they were very, very short. Then suddenly, the flashing of the computer screen caught Alana's eye. Emma moved in front of it, almost in defiance.

"What's going on, Mom?" Alana repeated quietly.

Emma slumped as if someone snatched away some invisible support, leaving her limp and defenseless.

"It was only meant to be a bit of fun … It was Katriona and Ling Ling's idea …"

At the sound of their names, Alana pushed her mother aside and read through the chat history between *PeterPan* and *LegsEleven.*

Alana looked up, eyes solemn. "You do realize he could be a serial killer. Or an alcoholic," she paused. "Or a dentist."

And so the next time Emma corresponded with *PeterPan,* she made it very clear. If he was any (or all) of those things, then their "relationship," such as it was, had to stop now. She wondered, with a guilty start, if she wasn't being a little bit hypocritical. After all, the words Widow, Single Mother and Writer remained untyped.

Instead, what they *did* write about was what they liked. (Emma: Waterfalls. Peter: Long motorbike rides through the forest.) What they didn't like. (Emma: Karaoke. Peter: Watching soccer – how could they play a whole match for 90 minutes and the score only be one-zero?) Their pet peeves.

(Emma: The sand that collects in the seat of your bikini bottom. Peter: Missing the buffet breakfast because you've slept in – come on, *five* different types of cereal.) What made them cry. (Emma: Almost everything. Even stupid commercials on TV when you know they're *acting*. Peter: Losing the family dog to cancer.) The best dessert they'd ever eaten … ever. (Emma: Tiramisu. No, it's not the name of an Italian city. Peter: Banana Cream Pie. Mom's, of course.) The most daring thing they'd ever done. (Emma: Shaved my head after a bad perm. Peter: Got a tattoo.) And their favorite read. (Emma: *The Importance of Being Earnest*. Peter: *Harry Potter*.)

The smiley emoticon alternately snored and winked, flashing on the screen.

PeterPan had signed off and gone to bed.

Emma sat dumbly in her chair.

Harry Potter???

CHAPTER 26

"Lah, lah, lah, lah, I DON'T WANT TO KNOW ABOUT IT!"

It was early on a Saturday evening, and the girls were at Alana's for a sleepover. All four were working on their homework. (This time, English. The fun and lightheartedness of the school holidays was already a distant memory.) It was the only place they could work in peace. Maddie's little brother and sister always wanted to play. Khalilah's mom was reaching a critical point in her thesis. This meant she was always jumping up to groom the cat, prepare a snack, or check on Khalilah's activities. Anything that stopped her from Getting Started – she had no idea a blank page could be so frightening. Sofia's brothers' latest obsession was seeing who could pee the furthest. So far, Dmitri declared himself winner, but the twins accused him of cheating by stepping over the line. The girls agreed boys were disgusting. Most boys. Except for Jet Tierbert.

"Listen to this, everybody," Sofia said, reading from her latest *Go Girl!* magazine, "Jet Tierbert likes long motorbike rides through the forest, but soccer fans, don't expect Jet to be cheering alongside you. It appears he can't stand watching the game. If you're a sleepyhead, chances are you will drive Jet Tierbert nuts. This guy hates to miss out on the lavish morning spreads found in hotels while on tour. He likes to make what he calls his special Cereal Surprise: all the cereals mixed together in the ONE BOWL! Oh Jet, you are one crazy cat! But the guitar-twanging rocker has a soft side. *Go Girl!* magazine correspondent, JuJu, caught him crying in the movie *Puppy Dog Blues*. Aww shucks, this guarantees Tierbert-ers will only love him more…" Sofia sighed as she put down the magazine. "He is too adorable!"

With a mouthful of warm, caramel popcorn, Khalilah agreed. "Even though he's not a soccer lover, I'd still like to be a passenger on one of his long bike rides in the forest –"

"– and ask him to go faster so you had an excuse to hold him tighter," Sofia winked, gripping a giggling Maddie's waist to demonstrate.

Alana quickly finished beading Maddie's hair before grabbing the magazine to read the rest of the article. If she didn't already have a good reason for not liking Jet Tierbert before, she certainly did now. How could he not appreciate the skill it took to play soccer? The footwork, the evasive maneuvering, the team strategy? And calling his pop efforts "rock" was an insult to every true rocker who ever lived. While the other girls wove colorful friendship bracelets, Alana read the article silently to herself.

Jet Tierbert is not only sweet, he also has a sweet-tooth. His all-time favorite dessert is his mom's banana cream pie, which he likes to eat while reading his favorite series, Harry Potter. Alana felt a familiar tingle, almost a shiver, in the back of her mind.

Something wasn't right.

Alana's mom, Emma, wandered into the living room, Katriona and Ling Ling hanging on to her every word.

"…so then I asked him what his favorite book was, and he said…"

"…*Harry Potter*," Alana said before she could stop herself.

Emma turned to look at her daughter in amazement. "That's right. He said, *Harry Potter*. How did you know?" she said, eyes wide.

Alana slid the magazine under a pile of books. Her hands were shaking. She hid those next. "Lucky guess, I guess."

"Yeah, I don't know. I feel a bit irked by that. I mean, *Harry Potter*? Should I feel icky? I feel icky."

Alana shook off the same feeling, and berated herself for an overactive imagination. Plenty of people rode a motorbike, hated soccer, and enjoyed buffet breakfast cereals. She was sure Sofia, now an avid collector of useless trivia, would say thousands of people cried in the same film and enjoyed banana cream pie. *But not all those things in the one person*, a tiny voice insisted. Jet Tierbert

= *PeterPan*?! It was ridiculous. Unthinkable. Illegal. What was he? Ten? Twelve? Alana checked the magazine. Sixteen. It was all a crazy coincidence. *But there's no such thing as coincidence,* the voice continued to taunt her. This time, there is, she growled. To believe otherwise was too awful.

Katriona was quick to point out that *Harry Potter* book covers came in two designs, one for adults and another for children. The series was popular with both – it was nothing to worry about. Lots of grown men liked *Harry Potter*.

"Absolutely," Alana agreed quickly, though struggling to imagine Uncle James or Mr. Hornby tucked up in bed with a copy.

"And his avatar is a cartoon caricature. Doesn't that strike you as odd?" Emma persisted.

"I would rather find out more about that tattoo of his. Like, *what* it is."

"Yeah, and *where* it is," Ling Ling said with a look full of meaning.

Katriona and Ling Ling were soon nudging each other and winking and laughing while Alana and her friends rolled their eyes.

"Hey, hey, I've got an idea, Emma, I've got an idea," Katriona cried. "Why don't *you* get a tattoo?"

Emma felt a sudden thrill. She'd always wanted one but could never decide what design, or where to put it.

"Yes, yes, why don't we ALL get one? We could get one that kind of fits together. So when we stand like this," Ling Ling said, demonstrating, "it will be one picture. See?"

"Or not … Maybe matching tattoos would be better! Otherwise when we're not standing Like This, it will look as if they didn't finish it. Yes, let's do it. I know a brilliant tattoo artist," Katriona said, eyes shining.

Katriona and Ling Ling were already holding hands and jumping up and down. Emma turned to Alana as if to ask for permission. But Alana didn't notice. She had closed her eyes, blocked her ears with her hands, and was singing at the top of her voice, "*Lah, lah, lah, lah,* I DON'T WANT TO KNOW ABOUT IT!"

Before Emma raced out the door, she arranged for a sitter, popped her Mexican *sombrero* on her head, and grabbed the spare change from a jar on the fridge. Then she threw open the freezer and shoved a block of ice in her bag … in case that wasn't enough.

CHAPTER 27

Tattoos, chickens, and botched translations.

Tony's Tattoos did not do tiny roses on shoulders, or mini-love hearts at the base of the spine. They did not do wreaths of flowers encircling fingers, wrists, or ankles, either. The art Tony and his crew did covered huge swathes of skin. Their pictures covered toes and traveled the length of legs, only to change direction and reappear mysteriously across the other side on a shoulder. Their usual canvas was whole backs, necks, and even faces. Tony himself had a tattoo of the map of St. Christopher's Cemetery. In case he needed it, he said. It covered his entire chest, a muscled torso of hairless bronze.

Emma found herself staring at the tombstone of a *Felicity Fairchild: Angel, beloved sister, and daughter, 1881 – 1882.* "The detail is amaaa-zing …" she whispered.

Tony stepped back slightly so Emma's head no longer nestled in his underarm. Ling Ling grabbed Emma's hand just in time, before it could touch the realistic outline of a tree. Katriona pointedly ignored her as she smiled and air-kissed the tattoo artist with loud *mwahs*.

"Tony! Dah-ling! It's been too long!"

"What can I do you for, Kat?"

Katriona gave a girlish giggle. "Actually, my friends and I are thinking about matching tattoos…"

Tony's eyes lit up. He rubbed his hands with delight. He crooked a finger and gestured for them to look at his computer screen, displaying a host of designs.

"I've been saving this one for you," he said, showing Katriona a picture of a leopard to cover her entire body. "I could do a dragon for your friend over there, and for her…" he said, looking at Emma speculatively, "maybe a rabbit."

"A rabbit!" Emma repeated in disgust.

"With fierce teeth. Really fierce," Tony said

with a buck-toothed *grrr.*

Tony of Tony's Tattoos led Katriona to a screened-off area, where she was invited to put on a robe. Ling Ling and Emma were placed in similar cubicles to do the same. Emma thought. *A rabbit on my skin. Forever.* Would she still like the rabbit tomorrow? Or next year? In ten years? A tattoo was not something you got rid of easily, or changed like a pair of shoes. The more Emma thought about it, the more she realized that maybe a tattoo wasn't for her. At least not the forever kind. And definitely not a rabbit, however fierce.

"Hi, umm, Guy," Emma said to the tattoo artist, who swished the curtains aside to enter the room. "I don't know if I want a *real* tattoo, you know what I mean? Maybe we could start off with one of those ones that wash off with water, or something? Do you have any of those?"

Guy, bald as the day he was born, with his head and the skin surrounding one eye inked in a complex design of machinery to make him look like a cyborg, grunted a no. He then grabbed her arm gently but firmly to begin the preliminary design. Later, he would retrace the lines, using a needle to pierce the skin, and then fill with color. Emma watched him work and marveled at his skill. She was almost tempted to go through with it until she heard the buzzing of the tattoo needle next door. It sounded just like a drill at the dentist's. Emma suppressed a shudder. She hated going to the dentist! But it was the rattle of the trolley that made up her mind, as a pile of blood-soaked gauze wheeled past. Ah yes. That was the other reason Emma had never got a tattoo. Her low threshold for pain. Very, *very* low.

Emma jumped up suddenly, taking Guy by surprise.

"I'm so sorry. I can't. It's beautiful artwork, but I just can't. You understand, don't you?"

Guy did. He had been in the tattoo business with Tony for many years, and if he knew anything, Emma was not the tattoo type. Even for a cute little bunny rabbit with Fierce Teeth.

Katriona was in the next room. When Emma

peeped in, she saw her friend lying on her tummy, hitting the bench with one hand.

"Stop! Stop! I can't take it," she shrieked. Tony raised his eyes to Emma's with Basset Hound resignation. "It's so TICKLISH!" A leopard's ears and eyes stared out from Katriona's back in washable ink. Tony had not managed to finish the design, much less start tattooing. Katriona continued to giggle.

"I'm going to the corner shop to grab some munchies. Won't be long."

"Take your time," Tony said somberly, as Katriona continued to snort. "It could be a long night."

Emma shivered as she navigated Darlinghurst's busy streets. The harsh fluorescent lights of convenience stores and take-away outlets hit the pavement in angled trapezoids. A "vacancy" sign flashed on and off, momentarily illuminating two couples like a stop-start film while they strolled hand in hand. That they had feather boas, five-inch heels and four Adam's apples between them didn't surprise her, but throwing coins at a busker, did. Even for the back streets of the city, it was a stretch to call it music. The musician was a short man with random tufts of hair on his head, pouches under his eyes, and cheeks darkened by stubble. He kept his eyes closed as if in a trance, and hit the top of a metal trash can with a stick. He was oblivious to the fact he was now eight dollars richer.

Bang. Bang. Bang. Bang.

"Shut up! Get outta here," yelled a voice from upstairs, before a shower of trash came raining down. A trash can lid followed as a further incentive to move, crashing down on the pavement and narrowly missing them both.

The busker opened his eyes. He reached out and tapped on the second lid. It was slightly higher in tone.

Bang. Bing. Bang. Bing. Bang. Bing.

Emma hurried forward before anything else came down. The winter air bit through the thin cotton of her top. She was thankful the Mexican hat covered her ears and most of her face. The corner store was not far away and not very large. With three or four aisles, it stocked the usual items people discovered a sudden need for at 3 o'clock in the morning. Emma bent down to check the label on a bag of organic chips. It promised less fat and less salt than its competitors. She added it to her pile, then transferred her shopping to one hand as she juggled her handbag open. She was sure she had enough coins to pay. And if that wasn't enough, she could always defrost her credit card.

It was Alana's idea that Emma's seven credit cards be reduced to one. And that that one credit card be frozen in a block of ice. After 450 copies of *Pride and Prejudice* had arrived last year, it seemed the only sensible thing to do. Emma blamed the confusion of online shopping for the mistake. The lovely man at the call center was very understanding. After he stopped laughing, he agreed to take it all back and cancel the transaction. Nevertheless, Emma's "spending money" was reduced to the spare change from a jar on the fridge (a bulky, clay urn which weighed a ton) and the large slab of ice for emergencies. Everything else was paid for by internet banking … which Alana, quite sensibly, controlled.

While Emma searched for a suitable drink to go with their snacks, she heard the tiny, silver bell above the front door of the corner store jangle. Somebody was yelling.

"This is a stickup. A stickup. Let me see your hands. Give me your money. I want everything. Everything in the register," a youth in a mask roared. He reached into his jacket and pulled out … a rubber chicken. This was not the Lethal Weapon he was expecting. He rushed to his accomplice who was guarding the door. A furious burst of whispering ensued. Today had been a Bad Day for them, full of miscommunications and mess-ups. The ill-chosen weapon was the last straw. Nevertheless, he rallied and returned to bang the rubber chicken on the counter.

"*Waaah!*" it wailed.

The shopkeeper, a small Asian man, continued

to play solitaire with apparent calm.

"Are you listening? Are you deaf? I said I want all your money in the register. NOW!"

The shopkeeper flipped over a card and tutted at the result. It seemed this was not the card he wanted.

"Look, if you don't mind, I'm in a bit of a rush. I'll just pay and leave you to it, shall I?" Emma explained with her most winning smile. The masked robber just looked at her in amazement.

"No one's leaving until I get the money!" he screamed, waving the floppy chicken about. "Explain. Tell him. Tell him if he doesn't give us all the money in the till, he's going to ... to ... get brained by the bird. TELL HIM!" The robber became more hysterical as the cashier sat, almost bored, and continued to play cards.

"C'mon, bro!" came a yell from the door. "Get a move on!" The robber on guard duty had an unusually thick neck. He fidgeted with the mask which was too small for his head and kept riding up.

"But I don't speak Chinese. I think … he only understands Chinese," Emma said, looking at the shopkeeper with uncertainty.

"*You* look Chinese. Kind of. Chinese-Mexican-ish," he said, taking in Emma's massive hat.

"I know, but I'm not. Everybody always says that. I think it's from my mother's side, you know? Anyway," she hastened to add as he gestured impatiently. "I don't speak Chinese. I'm from the Philippines. You know how we all look alike. Ha ha …" she said with false cheer, but the thief was not in the mood for irony. He was ready to implode. He changed his plan and asked for Emma's money instead. Emma held up the-spare-change-from-a-jar-on-the-fridge in one hand, and the block of ice in the other. "My daughter says I have spending issues …"

The thief swore in frustration. Then Emma – because she understood Work Stress – tried to help by miming the actions and speaking slowly and loudly to the now bemused shopkeeper.

Because, as any English-speaking tourist will tell you, if you speak slow enough, loud enough, and maintain good eye contact, eventually they'll understand.

"If you don't give him … him … this guy … yes … the money … he … will … hurt … you …" she shouted slowly, alternately bashing and strangling the borrowed rubber chicken. She finished off with a death scene of Last-Minute Farewells and Expressive Eyes.

"*Waaah!*" the rubber chicken wailed in sympathy.

Emma had always harbored a secret ambition to be an actress. By the time she'd finished swooning onto the floor, therefore, blood was everywhere, and the audience was in tears. But the only thing the shopkeeper saw was a couple of street performers. *Amateurs. Pah!*

A *ding! ding! ding!* from a mobile phone preceded a jaunty jingle promising soda, evoking a memory more powerful than the platypus and the surfer who sang it.

Hugo! Hugo's jingle was the robber's ringtone, Emma realized, amazed.

"Yes, Mom?" the masked male mumbled. "I'm a bit busy right now," he continued in an undertone.

Emma stayed dead as a woman's voice screeched a response.

"Yeah but … yeah okay, but … does it have to be now?" There was an unintelligible shriek. "Okay, okay, which one is it? … Yeah, okay then. I gotta go," he muttered, as he stomped a small distance away to check the shelves. From the corner of one barely open eye, Emma watched him choose a box of tampons, only to swap it for a "silky, cotton" brand. He stuffed it hastily into the pocket of his jacket and returned to the counter. Even through her now-tightly-shut eyelids, Emma could feel the waves of his frustration boiling over.

The second robber, who stood guard as if standing on hot coals, joined them. He looked at Emma's prostrate body, and the dead chicken beside her, while bouncing on the balls of his feet.

"What did you do?" he screamed.

The first robber looked down. "Nothing!"

His partner in crime rushed to the entrance to check that no one was coming. He returned almost instantly.

"Come on. Let's go. Forget it. We can try one up the road. This place sucks!"

His mate, almost tearful, agreed. "Yeah, this place sucks. You suck!" he yelled, picking up the rubber chicken and shoving it back into his jacket as he ran away.

Katriona and Ling Ling pushed open the door of the poorly lit corner shop almost as soon as the failed thieves had left. Emma, no longer dead, was counting out coins onto the counter in haphazard piles.

"What was all that about?"

"Apparently, I suck," Emma said thoughtfully, and then began again, having lost count.

"Yeah, well we do too. It was too ticklish to get the tattoo, and Ling Ling developed a strange tick. Her leg kept jerking every time he tried to draw."

Katriona and Ling Ling showed Emma the half-drawn masterpieces on their bodies.

It must be said that Emma's thespian performance did nothing to help her community lawyer who had to defend her later. Her mock threats with the rubber chicken on the surveillance tape looked dubious at best. Were an animal's rights being violated? In the end, the judge let Emma off with a warning, but suggested she refrain from translating heists in the future.

CHAPTER 28

Best birthday surprise... E-VER!!!

The sound of a violin plunking the first bars of "Happy Birthday" reached Alana before she could see who was playing. She knew, of course, it would be Maddie, and she was right. A flute joined in, and then a tamborine. By the time Alana entered her bedroom, the song was in full swing and the girls were playing in double time. It galloped its way to the finish.

"It's your birthday soon, isn't it, Alana?"

"Yes, Alana is a Virgo. A true perfectionist who needs everything in its spe-cial spot," Sofia said with a teasing grin. The other girls looked around at the neatness of Alana's bedroom. A bookshelf was fashioned out of an old skateboard. Notes for "Study schedules" and "Soccer practice" were pinned to a cork board. Curtains of crimson let in the morning light, lending the turquoise walls an even brighter glow. A framed photograph of a three year-old Alana and her frizzy-haired dad took pride of place by her bed. Both of them wore silly grins, sitting on the couch each with a guitar on their lap. Alana's sole homage to rock 'n' roll was a full-length silhouette cutout of Jimi Hendrix, above which was a quote from WC Fields: *Start each day with a smile – just get it over with.*

Alana gave a heartfelt sigh. "It's next week. The first of September. Please don't remind me."

"What's wrong?" Khalilah asked. "I love birthdays. You get presents, you're made to feel special, and there's cake! What's not to love?"

"Well, Alana's not had much luck with her birthdays," Maddie confided.

Alana silently passed Khalilah a photo album. The pictures explained why every birthday filled her with dread and foreboding. Khalilah turned the pages, expecting to see smiling faces, balloons, and festive food. Instead, dancing llamas munched on Alana's hat while it sat on her head. Preschool pirates were crying next to Peter Pan,

Captain Hook, and a very real croc. And "Harry Houtini," who h-escaped from h-everything, sat trapped, tangled and terribly visible, in a box. At least the circus-themed party looked like fun. Alana, in a furry hat, had a huge, toothy smile on her face. Khalilah looked more closely. Alana was not smiling. There was no hat. Against a backdrop of fire-breathing jugglers, a flea circus, and a unicyclist on stilts, Alana's mouth was open in a silent scream, hair on fire. Khalilah passed the photo album back, eyes round with shock.

"This year, Mom is being extremely tightlipped about it, *and* she's acting very excited. It's not a good sign."

"So you don't know what she has planned? At all?" Maddie asked. Alana shook her head.

"Maybe this year will be different."

"Sofia," Alana said, "what are the chances of my birthday NOT being a complete and utter fiasco this year?"

"Did you know 23% of all photocopier faults are caused by people sitting on them and photocopying their butts?"

"*Merci,* Sofia, for that fascinating fact, but please, just answer the question."

"It's tricky to calculate because of so many variables, but," with a look at Alana's raised eyebrow, "I'd have to say, judging from your mom's record and my new powers in probability … zero."

Alana sighed. "Yep. That's what I'd say, too."

The girls were together to hear the results of the Original Song Competition. The online poll was tight. For several days their song "Stormy Heart" had been neck and neck with the song "Forever Yours." The winning song was going on air at exactly 10 o'clock. The hands on the clock moved with agonizing slowness.

You're tuned to 95.9 FM, Double V. That was Rude Boy's latest song, "Breakdown." In just a few moments we'll find out the winner of our Original Song Competition, and I have to say, there is some incredible talent out there. All the entries were amazing. Our very deserving winners will get two free tickets to see Slam Guru, supported by

Jet Tierbert, in concert, PLUS backstage passes to meet the stars! Rumor has it, Jet will be debuting his new single during this tour, so if you already have tickets, look forward to that one. Now, to get you all in the mood, here's a little preview of what's to come ... from Jet Tierbert.

"I can't stand the suspense anymore!"

"Yeah, it's driving me crazy!"

"I know. Even *I'm* feeling a bit *nerveux*," said Alana.

"I don't know what that means, but I do know I'm so nervous I think I'm going to pee my pants," Sofia cried.

"I'm not that *nerveux*!" Alana said with a grin.

Then all four girls – even Alana, who had to admit that it *was* catchy – joined in with the radio. They danced and bounced around the room, yelling out the lyrics they knew by heart.

The clock's hand edged closer and closer. As the last chords of Jet Tierbert's song faded, and the girls' voices with it, the clock struck ten.

And now, the moment you've all been waiting

for. Our winning song …

Even before the first chords finished playing, the four girls were screaming. It was *their* song. Their song was on the radio!

Nyah, nyah, nyah, nyah, nyah (Drumsticks - One, two, three, four)

You think you can handle this?

Oh yeah … I don't think so.

"I can't believe it. We're on air. That's us on the radio!"

"Listen, listen, that's me on violin!"

"And here's Khalilah on flute!"

Then all of them stopped, and raised their hands, only to bring them crashing down again in an imitation of Sofia's drumming as the beat punched the speakers. *Boom, boom, boom, boom, boom,* they mimed. Alana beamed with satisfaction. You could turn any soppy love song into something decent with some proper, hardcore rock. Next, heads were tossing as they joined Alana on air guitar, before belting out the chorus.

Emma drifted out of her study and up the stairs

to join them. They'd made such a ruckus, even she couldn't ignore it.

"Mom, Mom, we're on the radio. That's us. We won the Original Song Competition!"

"We've won tickets to see Slam Guru –"

"– and Jet Tierbert in concert –"

"– and we're going to meet them ... BACKSTAGE!"

The four friends were thrown into a new paroxysm of delight as their excitement shifted from being on the radio to the winning prize. There was more screaming. Very loud. Very high-pitched. Enough to wake the dead, or at the very least, send the neighborhood dogs into hiding.

Emma wrapped her arms around Alana and gave her a big hug. "That's wonderful news, darling! You're so clever," she said into her daughter's ear so she could be heard. "But that's exactly what I was giving you for your birthday."

"What? That's it? Just concert tickets? Nothing on fire, or sharp, or death-defying?"

"Well, they *are* the hottest tickets around, and

I got backstage passes, too. AND an invite to the after party …"

Alana flung her arms around her mom and gripped her tight. "You're the best! And this is the best birthday surprise ever!"

CHAPTER 29

Ticket to happiness.

PeterPan: I've written you a song.

LegsEleven: Really? Let's see it then.

PeterPan: Promise you won't laugh.

LegsEleven: I promise you won't know it if I do.

PeterPan: LOL. OK. Here goes …

I'm not a serial killer … unless you'd want me to die for you, baby.

I'm not an alcoholic … I'm just drunk on our love.

And if you said the word, then I would be your nerd, because you glue me to my screen.

I'm just a puppet on your string, and you're pulling so I cling

To every little word you say.

Just say. I need you today.

So what do you think?

LegsEleven: You forgot "dentist."

PeterPan: That's because I have a confession to

make.

Emma felt her heart drop. This was it. Surely this was when he revealed he was The Frog and not The Prince?

LegsEleven: What's your confession?

PeterPan: I AM a dentist.

LegsEleven: You're what?!

PeterPan: Kidding. Did you like it?

LegsEleven: It's probably one of the sweetest things anybody has done for me.

PeterPan: Can we meet?

Emma hesitated. Her hands hovered above the keyboard, suspended like a tightrope walker before their first step.

LegsEleven: Do you think that's a good idea?

PeterPan: Nothing too scary. Somewhere public and fun. No strings.

LegsEleven: Like …?

PeterPan: I was thinking … I can get you a couple of tickets to the Slam Guru concert and backstage passes. We can meet there. See where it goes …

LegsEleven: Really? You must have connections.

They've been sold out for months.

PeterPan: I know a guy who knows a guy … you know how it is. We could both wear a rose ;) So what do you think? Are you willing to take a chance?

Emma bit her lip. She didn't need the tickets, but she knew accepting them would mean all of Alana's friends could go. Which she knew would make them incredibly happy. Katriona and Ling Ling could flip a coin to decide who would get the spare. Plus, maybe her friends were right. Maybe she *should* start dating again. And she could always use Alana's birthday as a quick getaway excuse. Yes. She would just shake his hand, say *Hi, nice to meet you*, and if there was some spark that made her heart skip a beat, she could arrange to meet him again. Emma gave a self-conscious laugh. She'd been listening to too many of the girls' love songs.

When Alana came home from soccer practice, Emma sat her down to talk about the concert, and what she had planned.

"I swear I'm just going to say hi, and if things work out, then we could always meet properly another time. This is your birthday. And I want it to be special," she said, but Alana wasn't listening. All she heard was "free ticket, *blah, blah, blah,* all your friends can go, *blah, blah, blah,* birthday, *blah, blah, blah.*" Which proves selective hearing is not an adult's privilege alone.

Without waiting for her mom to finish, Alana rushed to share the good news.

...

Katriona and Ling Ling watched the coin fall for the twentieth time.

"Tails."

"Heads."

"What?"

"I win again, Katriona."

"No, this is impossible. This coin is rigged. I MUST HAVE THIS TICKET!"

"Please let go of my neck, Katriona. I have an idea ..."

CHAPTER 30

Best birthday surprise...
E-VER!!!... *Not!*

Emma placed the finishing touches on Alana's birthday cake, which was shaped like an electric guitar. She was glad nobody had been home to watch her assemble it. It was amazing what two pounds of icing could do to cover up mistakes. Thirteen candles stood in a long line on one of the guitar "strings." The flames flickered as Emma lifted the cake and brought it through to the living room, where their closest friends were waiting.

Happy Birthday to you,

Happy Birthday to you,

Happy Birthday dear Alana/Lala/Lana-Banana, the voices chorused. Alana narrowed her eyes at Katriona. She was sure she'd heard someone sing, *"Piranha"*...

Happy Birthday to you!

Hip, hip, hooray! Hip, hip, hooray! Hip, hip, hooray!

Alana closed her eyes and blew out the candles as she made her silent wish. Everybody burst into applause. James snapped madly with his camera.

Looking around at their smiling faces, Alana was overcome by a sudden wave of mixed emotions. "Thanks for coming, everyone," she mumbled, tearing up.

"Toughen up, Princess," Maddie chided softly. The warmth and sympathy in her ocean-blue eyes softened the words. Alana gave her a sheepish grin full of gratitude.

"You already know mine," Emma said with a smile, cutting slabs of chocolate guitar, pegs, and strings, and giving them out.

"This is from me," Sofia said, handing Alana a small box with a flourish. "I know you will use it wisely."

Inside was a Magic 8 Ball. The four girls laughed.

"Khalilah and I got you this," Maddie said as Khalilah passed her a soft, flat package. It was a T-shirt. Alana held it up for everyone to see. *Rock Chicks Rock … Duh!* the front of it read.

"Thanks. It's perfect! I'll wear it tonight for the

concert." Alana grinned.

James was next. "This is from me." The box was small and light. Alana gave a squeal of delight when she opened it. "I'm not a fan of point-and-shoot cameras," he said ruefully, "but they come in handy."

Emma smiled. Point-and-shoot cameras were the only kind she used. "You can use it underwater too, which will be fun for the summer."

Ling Ling dragged Katriona over. "We didn't know what to get you, Alana, so we decided on a pet." Everybody stared at the pair. Didn't they know they were giving the animal a death sentence?

"Thanks, Auntie Ling Ling, but I don't think –"

Katriona shoved the package in her arms as Alana muttered a "thanks." Alana lifted the lid slightly and held her breath. What could it be? A second kidnapped penguin? A venomous snake? Something on the endangered wildlife list? Whatever it was, the disaster was right on time. When Alana removed the lid completely, she breathed a sigh of relief as she read the message:

Hi! I'm Rocky, your pet rock. I love listening to rock 'n roll and eating rock candy. Don't forget to rock me to sleep! Love, R x

Alana gave Ling Ling a hug and, because Katriona baulked at the same gesture, gave her a pat on the arm.

"We thought it would be hard for your mom to kill this one," Ling Ling whispered, then turned to everyone. "Time to get ready for Slam Guruuuuuuuuuuu!" She exchanged a meaningful wink with Katriona. "See you later," she mouthed.

Alana's heart stopped. There were only enough tickets for the seven of them. What did *that* mean?

...

As Emma got ready for the concert, she swiveled from side to side, checking her profile in consternation. *PeterPan* was expecting to meet *LegsEleven,* not Emmalina Estafania Corazon Oakley, widowed writer, mother of one. But

Chapter 30

Emma Oakley looked nothing like *LegsEleven*. If she squinted with one eye, *LegsEleven* looked like a slightly older Alana. Well, Emma sighed, I hope this does the trick. The Trick, she was referring to, was her new outfit, which promised to give her curves.

Alana walked into her mom's bedroom.

"What do you think? Too much?" Emma asked, continuing to twist her body, this way and that, in front of the mirror.

"Let's go!" she beamed at Alana with false cheer. Truth be known, she was shaking inside.

The crowd at the Sydney Cricket Ground was huge. Most of them had bought, or were buying, Slam Guru and Jet Tierbert CDs, T-shirts, programs, and other souvenirs. Hardcore rockers milled around with giggling pre-teens. The gig had drawn an eclectic mix of fans. Emma's freebies and the girls' prize saw them seated in the same area as the entertainment press and designated VIPs. They were so close to the stage, they were bound to be sweated on. This knowledge gave

Ling Ling an extra thrill. Emma waved to a couple of reviewers she recognized. Alana and her friends shuffled forward impatiently.

"Tickets, please," a strangely familiar pair of Jimmy Choo's requested.

Alana looked up from the bright, fashionable shoes, which didn't quite match the security guard's uniform.

"Auntie *Katriona?*"

"Your tickets, please," the voice repeated, in a deeper tone.

Alana turned to her mom in alarm. A panicked whispering ensued. The security guard's resolve seemed to waver as they joined in the heated argument.

A second security guard joined the first, to ask, "Is there a problem?"

"No! No problem. Everything's A-OK," Katriona said (for Alana was right), heartily slapping the beefy man on his back, then lightly punching a bicep, which was pushing the fabric to its limits. The resulting pain brought a tear to her eye.

Perhaps it was her not-so-deep voice which gave Katriona away. Or the bright red, high-heeled shoes. Or it could have been the identification tag which read *Sekurity* in smudgy, barely dry ink (*Sekurity, security, same-same, lah!*). But whatever it was, Mr. Beefy was suddenly shouting, "Code Red. I repeat, Code Red! Mayday! Mayday! DEFCON 1 Alert!" into a slim walkie-talkie.

Katriona's eyes swiveled around for the threat. She was a jaguar, ready to pounce. She scanned the excited masses for danger. "Wha-? Where? Who? Let me at them!" she growled.

Six Mr. Beefy look-a-likes charged toward them. They swept Katriona off her feet. She'd imagined that at some stage during the concert she'd be crowd surfing, but certainly not this early. Not before she'd even heard Slam Guru sing one note. The guards lifting Katriona's rear grunted and strained with the effort.

"Hey! *Hey!*" she protested, as she was propelled

further and further away from the show. This was NOT part of The Plan!

Suddenly, the lights dimmed as the stadium prepared for the first performance of the night. Jet Tierbert.

The crowd surged forward. Thousands of voices screamed Jet's name.

"Hello Sydneyyyyyyyy!" A voice echoed all around them.

The response was deafening. Alana and Emma shared a grin as they covered their ears. Maddie, Sofia, Khalilah, and Ling Ling were screaming and jumping up and down. The stage burst into an explosion of color and bright lights, flashing to the beat of Jet's first song, while Jet himself jumped off a high podium to land with cat-like grace, microphone at the ready. He slicked back his bangs and belted out the first verse before throwing the microphone to a waiting stagehand and joining dancers in a tightly choreographed routine that had the front rows swooning. Within minutes the stadium was transformed into a heaving pit of writhing bodies, sweaty and carefree as people abandoned themselves to the music. The next song was equally upbeat, and then the energy ramped up even more when he sang with a local guest rapper. Then, just when they thought they could take no more, Jet sat down on a stool in the middle of the stage, alone with an acoustic guitar. A single spotlight threw shadows onto his face. His dark bangs hung long and low. As he crooned his ballad "Don't Leave Me," many, like Sofia, were in tears. Jet stopped singing and held the microphone out for fans to sing. *So don't leave me, please. How can it be over before it's begun? Walking away from what could have been. O-ver, when we're not done.* Emma had her arms around Alana and they swayed to the gentle rhythm, singing with the crowd. Alana hated to admit it, but Jet Tierbert was pretty good … for a pop star.

"Best birthday. E-VER!" Alana mouthed.

Emma glowed with happiness.

All too soon it was over, and then it was Slam Guru on stage, doing what he does best: entertain.

Alana and her friends threw themselves into the rock-and-roll beats. Not to be left out (or left behind), Emma and Ling Ling raised their arms and pumped the air, bashing and shaking hips. It was a high-octane performance, with light shows and dancers and aerialists. They screamed until their voices were hoarse. Bodies floated on a sea of hands close to the stage. Ling Ling, swept up in the moment, threw herself into the throng and, likewise, was borne away – a fluorescent stick figure that became a distant speck.

To Sofia's delight, Slam Guru's percussionist launched into a drum solo accompanied by flashes of fireworks on stage. Faster and faster his sticks flew, his hands a blur. And then they slowed. Slowed, slowed, and stopped. Until only the deep *boom* of the kick drum, measured and deliberate, could be heard. He raised his hands in a "V" and brought them together. His dark silhouette urged fans to clap along. The crowd complied. He took off his T-shirt, sweaty and torn, and flung it into the masses. They screamed. The beat built up speed, faster and faster. Faster and faster, still. When it was almost one note, with no gap in between, a burst of fire illuminated Slam Guru on stage. His guitar was raised in the air. One arm swept down along the strings. The dramatic *thrum* signified the start of his latest hit. The crowd yelled in recognition. Wild, but not yet worn out, they sang along to this final song. Fifty thousand voices rose to the heavens. After the third encore, Slam Guru held his hands out for quiet. Big, bold rings glinted like fire in the stage lights.

"Who wants to hear more from that weedy guy who was out here before?" he said with a smile.

Tierbert fans went wild. They couldn't believe their luck. Jet was performing again?

"He's like a little brother to me. And when he said he wanted to sing a special song, to a special someone he's hoping is in the audience right now," – Slam Guru paused dramatically, the audience held their breath – "how could I say no? So here he is, Sydney, with his latest song, never before sung, you're hearing it here first, Jet Tierbert!"

The young heart-throb returned to the stage to deafening applause and catcalls.

"This one's for you, *LegsEleven!*"

Then the teenager, almost shyly, began the first chords of his song, the beginning of which was almost drowned out by adoring fans …

I'm not a serial killer … unless you'd want me to die for you, baby.

I'm not an alcoholic … I'm just drunk on our love.

And if you said the word, then I would be your nerd, because you glue me to my screen.

I'm just a puppet on your string, and you're pulling so I cling

To every little word you say.

Just say. I need you today.

Emma felt her knees buckle almost as fast as her excitement. She suddenly found it hard to breathe. She knew those words. How could Jet Tierbert be singing those words? UNLESS *PETERPAN* WAS JET TIERBERT. Emma squashed the thought before it could even gain flight. It was ridiculous. Unthinkable. Illegal. What was he? Ten? Twelve?

"Sixteen," Alana's answer broke into Emma's thoughts.

"OMG, I'm old enough to be his mother."

Alana sat down heavily next to her. "Crud," she said.

Then, because Emma appreciated a good joke, especially one played on herself, she laughed and shook her head. "Your French is coming along well." The pair collapsed into a heap of giggles. Emma reached out to smooth her daughter's flyaway hair, so like her own, which stuck out at odd angles. "Happy thirteenth, Alana."

"Thanks Mom. It's been the best birthday, ever."

"Oh, stop. I messed it up again."

"It wouldn't be *my* birthday if there wasn't *some* drama … But I betcha Dad's peeing himself laughing over *this* one! Pardon my French again."

Emma and Alana looked up into the heavens, visible above the open-air stadium, and grinned. A tiny star, much brighter than the others, seemed to twinkle back.

…

Mr. Beefy returned. "Excuse me? I'm here for the Original Song winners and *LegsEleven*. You have backstage passes? This way, please …"

Emma, giving Alana a not-so-gentle push, said, "*LegsEleven?* Here she is," and mouthed a Sorry, Terribly Sorry, to her daughter, whose face was full of panic.

"Mo-o-o-o-o-o-o-m!" Alana wailed.

Backstage, with a yellow rose newly pinned to her *Rock Chicks Rock …Duh!* T-shirt, Alana waited with her friends, who were twittering like a flock of parakeets. The girls' excitement was palpable. Her mom was already caught up in a lively conversation with James and Slam Guru, but she took time to give Alana a thumbs-up and a wink. If looks could kill, Emma would have been sushi. *You can do this,* Alana said to herself, and then faltered as Jet's face came into view. He was scanning the girls' outfits for a yellow rose. His own rose was clenched between his teeth, like a Spanish dancer preparing to tango. At the sight of Alana, the flower hit the floor. It was obvious he was expecting someone older. But he recovered in seconds and smoothly introduced himself, shaking hands with them all. Jet did most of the talking. Everyone else was too star-struck and tongue-tied, although it was for a very different reason that Alana kept quiet. While Sofia, Maddie, and Khalilah each chose a free autographed souvenir T-shirt, Jet sidled up to Alana for a private talk.

"You look a lot … *younger* than your avatar," he said.

"You look a lot more alive than yours," Alana swiftly retorted.

They both laughed and the initial awkwardness faded away. Alana had to hand it to Jet as they chatted. He *was* sweet. And funny. And even a little bit *mignon.*

"Here," she said, grabbing his guitar suddenly while her friends' mouths dropped like Venus Flytraps. "Let me show you how to *really* play this thing."

EPILOGUE

The water turned choppy as the charter boat moved farther from the outer reef. Before, it had been as flat as glass, reflecting the thin skein of cloud stretched across the sky like a bold brush-stroke. Now, white-tipped waves churned and frothed atop a rich turquoise blue that turned darker in deeper waters. The salty smell of the sea sizzled in the air. The boat's passengers looked forward to its blessed coolness, just one step away. The engine cut off. The boat slowed and stopped.

The *thunk* and *splash* of the step ladder as it was tipped over the side gave Slam Guru a jolt of excitement. After months of touring, he welcomed the "downtime" of snorkelling with Jet and his music crew. It was also exhilarating to be without his bodyguards. He was thousands of miles from Sydney on the west coast of Australia, at Ningaloo Reef. He felt safe enough here.

These waters were famous for their rich sea life, and Slam couldn't wait to see it. The boat rocked unsteadily as snorkelers shifted to the back of the boat. Some of them spat in their masks, using their saliva and a swirl of seawater to give them a clean. Others made a great show of delicately dabbing a bit of toothpaste to do the same. Jet gave a noisy hack and spat gustily with a huge grin. The teenager was riding a wave of happiness. Not only was this his first sea adventure Down Under, he'd finished his latest song "Just Friends," which was sure to be another hit. *Funny how life plays tricks ...* he hummed to himself.

Daniela, the tour leader, described the snorkeling plan.

"There's a light current today so the boat will drop us off here and pick us up over there," she said, indicating a point 100 meters away. "You can expect to see the usual big stuff: manta rays, dolphins, turtles, and dugongs, or sea cows, as they are also known."

"How about whale sharks?" Slam's music producer called out.

"Sorry, we're too late for the whale shark

season," she answered.

Jet laughed. "Phew, that's a relief. I didn't sign up for *Jaws.*"

"Relax. Whale sharks are not the bite-your-leg-off variety. They're filter feeders, so they're more interested in plankton than eating any of you," she said with a smile. "If you get cold, raise your arm and the boat will pick you up," she said, demonstrating. Then Daniela demonstrated some of the typical hand signals they could use with each other to communicate in the water.

Jet looked with impatience at the sea. He wanted to dive in right now. It was so clear – he could see schools of fish darting about. If he looked hard enough, he could almost see the *scales* on the schools of fish. When Daniela *did* give the "go" signal, it was Jet who beat everybody into the water, dive bombing with an excited cry. He dipped his head in and looked up with a yell to Slam, "Come on, bro. Get in here. It's awesome!"

But it wasn't only Jet who was excited. The skipper saw a familiar shadow, large and spotted, up ahead.

"Are you sure?" Daniela asked, brow furrowed. When he confirmed it, she raised her voice to grab their attention. "Milo has just said he's seen what looks to be a whale shark! This is an incredibly rare sighting, so we're very lucky. But before we follow it up, I need to lay down the ground rules. Adults can get up to 20 meters in length. If you get hit by one of those, it will feel like being run over by a tour bus, so give them plenty of room." The snorkelers laughed. "That means at least 3 meters on either side of the animal and 4 meters from its tail. Absolutely no touching, no riding, and no underwater flash photography, please." She looked around. "If no one has any questions, let's go."

Slam Guru's powerful strokes took him swiftly to the site Milo pointed at. Jet was not far behind. Slam signaled his intention by pointing his fingers at his mask and then the sea: he was going to scout the area for the whale shark. Jet nodded and copied the gesture. He would do the same. Slam veered slightly to the left, while Jet took off in the opposite direction. Slam's heart pumped fast. It wasn't the exertion, but his excitement and anticipation. He'd always wanted to see a whale shark, and swim with one even more. With the awkward timing of his tour, he thought he would miss the season, but it seemed luck was on his side. Slam took in the colorful fish, the turtles, and even the manta rays only in passing. With a promise to look at them later, he swam on. He was a hunter – a hunter of one of the ocean's most gentle giants. And he would hunt it down with his camera. Slam checked the flash was off. He didn't want to hurt the animal in any way.

In that split second, Slam caught sight of a large shadow far below him. He took a deep breath and dived in pursuit, painfully aware whale sharks could dive much deeper than he could. Down. Down. Down he went. He prayed his luck (and his lungs) held a little longer.

But what was this? As Slam got closer, the shape of the dark form changed. It became distorted. Misshapen. Bursting from the murky interior was a sight that chilled him to the bone. Slam reversed direction, kicking his powerful legs to propel himself upwards. Progress was agonizingly slow. He'd dived too far down. His lungs were bursting. He could barely see the light of the surface, but he couldn't give up. He'd gone from being The Hunter to The Hunted, and The Thing was in pursuit.

Finally, the darker blues of the deeper water gave way to lighter hues. Water dripped off the sides of Slam's mask and hair as he ripped off the snorkel. He took in a painful lungful of air. The other snorkelers had drifted with the current and were far away, weaving serenely through the water. Oblivious to the danger facing Slam Guru. Oblivious to his doom.

Slam Guru started toward the other swimmers, faint blobs in the distance. Something grabbed his leg from below. Slam panicked. He took off with a burst of speed, only to be seized with a cramp, which crippled his calf. With a gurgle of despair, Slam faced the terror he knew to be behind him.

"It's okay, Slam, I've got you," Katriona said as she reached lovingly for the panic-stricken rock star.

That's what I'm afraid of, thought Slam as he was flipped over expertly and placed in the rescue position. His throat was too choked from sea water to cry for help.

When they reached the boat, Milo and Jet, who'd returned for his camera, helped Katriona lift Slam's body out of the water.

As Slam Guru lay exhausted on the boat's bench, he made frantic "danger" hand signals, none of which Jet understood. Again and again his hand sliced along his throat. Jet brought him a glass of water for his "sore throat."

The terror in Slam's eyes grew as he watched Katriona Karovsky put her diving equipment down and walk toward him. This mystified Milo, who couldn't understand where the extra diver had come from.

"You're looking a bit peaky," she murmured. "I'd

better give you mouth-to-mouth resuscitation."

Slam Guru, eyes on stalks, watched Katriona's lips sashay toward him. They closed in until the rest of the world disappeared.

Milo nudged Jet and winked. "Lucky bloke, that one," he said.

"Lucky, alright," Jet agreed, eyeing Slam's flailing arms under Katriona's curvaceous form. *Lucky it's not me,* he shrugged, returning to the water's cool embrace.

Alana Oakley

BIOGRAPHY

Poppy Inkwell writes a lot of different things.

Stories...

Website content...

Mandalas...

But not Christmas cards ... or not very often.

When she's not at her desk writing, you will find her ferreting in car boot sales, experimenting with food gastronomy, or playing with her camera.

Born in the Philippines, she now lives by the beach in Australia with one husband, two of her children, and four pets (May They Rest In Peace).

See www.poppyinkwell.com for news and behind-the-scene-sneakpeeks of Book Two – *Alana Oakley: Torment and Trickery.*